She lies because I’m incarcerated…

PERIOD

She lies because I'm incarcerated...PERIOD

TANDT

ISBN-979-8-218-28034-5

DEDICATION

GOD FIRST!!! Thank YOU DEAR FATHER GOD!!! Thank YOU for allllll of YOUR WONDERFUL BLESSINGS!!! Thank YOU for Blessing Me with My AWESOME Wife & Kids. Smile=0) "Nola," thank You Queen. Trust, We know exactly who We are, and what We have been through to get to where We deserve to be.

Regardless of the "destination," as long as I have GOD, You, & our Kids... LETS GO, WE GOT THIS!!! Bae, "keep Your head to the sky" (Sounds Of Blackness/Optimistic). Thank You Nola... I could NOT have done this book without Your Love, Support, Patience, & Loyalty. I LOVE YOU FOREVER MRS. NOLA HSAAF!

This book, & the custom designed book cover is just a small portion of the super talented silhouettes that shine soooo BRIGHT, within prisons, worldwide.

No matter who you are, or what you may be currently incarcerated for, just know that GOD LOVES YOU! Please TRY to stay within positive lanes... no matter what race or religion you firmly believe in... WE ARE PRAYING FOR YOU-ALL, SINCERELY.

May this book be a small piece of motivation,

that will add up to be a HUGE PIECE OF ELEVATION, AMEN!!!

Never forget:

"A talented person is a talented person, no matter where you put them." {Pharrell Williams}

GOD-LOVE-PEACE

TANDT FOREVER!!!

Meet-an-Inmate.com (FOREVER!!!)

READ THIS ENTIRE BOOK
READ THIS ENTIRE BOOK
READ THIS ENTIRE BOOK
READ THIS ENTIRE BOOK
READ THIS ENTIRE
READ THIS ENTIRE BOOK
READ THIS ENTIRE BOOK
READ THIS ENTIRE BOOK
READ THIS ENTIRE BOOK
READ THIS
GOD
LOVE
READ THIS
BOOK
READ THIS ENTIRE
FREE
BOOK
READ THIS ENTIRE
READ THIS ENTIRE BOOK
READ THIS ENTIRE BOOK
READ THIS ENTIRE BOOK READ

No matter how good of a book I was reading... I often found myself falling into a quick daydream escaping my current situation, only to reminisce back into my past briefly. "Damn... I was ah fly ass dude... I was on my way... two old school BIG BODY CHEVYS, paid fo, switch'n rentals err week, hit'n da mall up err day, and switch'n women up like I did my clothes and sneakers. It was only right that I broke bread wit my real day ones... I was on my way... damn... I was on my way." I calmly thought to myself. That was me, (Adore Hsaaf) in the summer of 2003, but this is Me (Adore H. Robinson #345915) now, in the summer of 2004, an inmate currently being housed within the "Norfolk city jail."

My unorthodox daydream was interrupted by loud shouts and shit talk'n from fellow inmates. As I laid back on the bunk inside the cell, the hot temperature added to my mental torture, along with loud shouts. "Hold up-- hold up Young'n... read that last part one mo time!" A raspy baritone voice yelled. Young'n now had everyone's listening ears, including mine. "She said, 'I'on give ah fuck about you clown! So there, there you have it! Now... um bout to do something yo sorry ass can't do even if you wanted to. Um bout to walk outside and get some fresh air and enjoy my freedom!!' " Young'n shouted with clarity.

You could hear a pin drop... everyone momentarily paused... silently. "Damn Young'n... she ain't have to cut you that deep bruh, that's crazy, that bitch wrong for that!" That same raspy baritone voice, broke the silence.

I remained quite and laid back in awe on the bunk, with my book now laying flat on my chest, and thinking to myself... "damn... what would make her say something like that?"

After I was wrongfully convicted and sentenced to serve 28 years, I quickly began to mentally prepare myself to serve that time. I was 25 years of age when I was incarcerated. Prior to November 2003, I had NEVER been incarcerated. I worked as a licensed barber and recorded music on my spare time. For the most part... I was a "productive citizen." Harking back, I wasn't shy of having a plethora of female friends. However, its no surprise that depending on who you are/what you were/or, (and) the amount of incarceration time you have to serve... some of your "friends" on the outside, may move on without even reaching out to you.

In my case it was the contrary, but it didn't take long to recognize that most of my female friends were only reaching out because they simply could, and not with genuine love, support, or honest concerns. I quickly figured out how to deal with my "friends" on the outside. I invested my physical and my mental into a plethora of activities to keep busy, like cutting hair, working in the law library, fighting my own legal case, exercising, and last but never the least, MAKING TIME TO ACKNOWLEDGE GOD, which is a necessity for me. The first ten years of my incarceration time flew by with posthaste speed.

I made a promise to myself, that had I not been released legally by the time I got down to approximately ten years, then, I would focus more on accomplishing goals to show for myself during my incarceration, with hopes to stay within positive lanes upon my release from prison. Writing music, poems, drawing, painting, designing, creating custom logos, etc., are all awesome gifts GOD Blessed me with.

I would later learn that within the art realm, I'd be considered a "natural," or (and) a "freehand artist." Writing, drawing, painting, etc., became therapeutic for me during my incarceration. Don't get me wrong, I still communicated with my "female friends," even though the roster changed up frequently. Every once in a while, someone would pop back up from years ago... "same shit different day." Around 2017/2018, I had my nephew (Qwez) set up an IG page to showcase my drawings and paintings. A couple of years after, my IG page was "hacked." Unfortunately, that negated my inspiration to create any other social media pages to showcase my arts before my release date.

In 2021, I met a cool white guy (Chris) from Chesapeake Virginia, and like myself, Chris is also a "sneaker head." Lts (longer to shorter). We were chop'n it up one afternoon about "SNEAKER FREAKER," etc., when Chris asked nonchalantly, "a Hsaaf, I know you on one of dem sites, which one you on?" "What site... what I miss, or should I say what am I miss'n!?" I asked anxiously. "Member that lil chick wit da blond hair you said was 'cute,' da other day, da one I showed you on my music player?" I shook my head tacitly implying yes.

"Well... I met her on this site called 'Meet-an-Inmate,' you ah lock to find a female friend up there, matter fact, um bout to show you my profile on paper so you can see it for yourself!" Chris stated excitedly. Honestly, as soon as I locked down in the cell that same night, I anxiously proceeded to write down the site's information. The very next morning I got up early and called my nephew to inform him about "Meet-an-Inmate.com," Qwez wasted no time with helping me set up my profile on line. A few weeks later, Chris was released from prison.

Healthy communication is a necessity within my realm of reality. The Staff at Meet-an-Inmate are very respectful and professional. The wrong words spoken or written could determine my future business ventures with a company, organization, etc., and vice versa. The wrong words spoken or written on my behalf, could determine how a company, organization, etc., may or may not want to carry on any future business ventures with me.

The Staff @ Meet-an-Inmate.com, have no control over the personal personalities associated with the people whom may contact you once your profile is active. If you are not receiving any replies back within a respectful and timely manner, just inform the Staff ASAP, and I can assure you that the Staff will do whatever they can to help you with your profile.

Don't forget, "a closed mouth don't get fed," (in other words) if you don't inform the Staff, don't just expect the Staff @ Meet-an-Inmate.com to automatically know your problem(s). Only you, and not your "family" or "friends" can write the Staff, concerning your current situation.

In regards to all of the men and women that are able to use Meet-an-Inmate.com's platform to meet people, PLEASE TRY YOUR BEST NOT TO SHOWCASE ANY POPPYCOCK. Meet-an-Inmate is a professional business with awesome Staff that go above and beyond to help us, (the incarcerated).

I am a heterosexual male (with the utmost respect for everyone that may be homosexual, bisexual, etc.) These next few sentences are directed towards all of the women on the outside, within society, that reach out to heterosexual men, (such as myself) that are incarcerated. Ladies, please try to keep in mind that we, (the incarcerated) have REAL FEELINGS!

If you are reaching out or thinking about reaching out to someone currently incarcerated, please do not think that a person's incarceration status automatically makes him/her "inferior" to you, NOT! If someone within the moving society reaches out to an incarcerated person, please do not think that you are "superior" over that incarcerated person, NOT! I wanted to make that clear, because this book was partially wrote due to that same type of negative energy from ignorant people on the other side, within the moving society.

I personally feel that if you are a mature adult that may be incarcerated and looking for a mature woman or man within the moving society... Meet-an-Inmate.com is the best help for you, super fact, PERIOD. Part of my actual profile reads:

Name: Adore H. Robinson #345915

Current Prison Address: ???

[I'm an easy-going guy, I would prefer a positive energy, drama free, intelligent, GOD Fearing Woman. I love music, drawing, & painting!] Etc.

{The names and places used within this book, have all been changed to protect the actual individuals and locations. Therefore, if you "think" or, are "sure" that I am directly speaking about you in this book, YOU ARE WRONG! I am NOT speaking, talking, typing, etc., about you, so please... STOP IT! LOL!}

Due to the fact that I wasn't shy of having a plethora of "female friends" before my incarceration began back in November 2003, I was already somewhat familiar with the different finessing styles of most women, in regards to their lies and truths. I just "play possum." Basically, I listen, and I listen and I listen... I listen allllllll the way up until the point comes when I can't take the lies anymore. I let you think that I am blind to your poppycock, and then, depending on how my day is going... I give it to you--I can give it to you casually, or, I can give it to you so raw and uncut that it may cause you to be so "ANGRY" with me that your once fake "love" that you claimed to have had for me, quickly turns into "HATE." Mainly because most weak-minded people can't stand to be faced with the truths, especially when the truths are pointed directly at themselves, a silhouette of their own wrong doings.

This is a fact, and also one of many other reasons why I like to enter into a females "friendship"/ "relationship" etc., with authenticity, 100% AUTHENTICITY, PERIOD! If you continue to speak, type, etc., a bunch of small lies... then eventually you will be made out to be exactly what you are, ONE BIG LIAR!!! No, not all women... but some... okay, most women, there---I said it, because its true. The majority of the women that I have encountered before and during my incarceration, have turned out to be BIG LIARS, especially since I've been incarcerated, PERIOD. LOL!

READ THIS ENTIRE BOOK
READ THIS ENTIRE BOOK
READ THIS ENTIRE BOOK
READ THIS ENTIRE
READ THIS ENTIRE BOOK
READ THIS ENTIRE BOOK
READ THIS ENTIRE BOOK
READ THIS ENTIRE BOOK
READ THIS
READ THIS ENTIRE
READ THIS ENTIRE BOOK
READ THIS ENTIRE BOOK
READ THIS ENTIRE BOOK READ
GOD
LOVE
FREE
BOOK
THIS ENTIRE BOOK READ

Here are a few messages from various women I have communicated with during some of my time incarcerated, all the way up to the very moment I decided to have my profile placed on Meet-an-Inmate.

Sonya: "I'm up now getting ready for work, thank you for the card. It was really nice. I got two cards from you. One by email and one by mail. I attached a picture. I'm going to try to attach a picture every time I type you a letter. Much love, love you for life." (5/07/15)

Tonya: "Thank you for the birthday wishes. I appreciate it. My birthday was real nice and quiet with the family. I am blessed and I thank God daily for EVERYTHING." (4/05/16)

Shereka: "Hey babe... hope all is well=0) I just got finished rereading the very powerful message you sent me! Its really deep and touched me as I read it=0) You have always been 100% with me and I Love that and other things about you! Thanks for spending the weekend with me, and also for the cards, etc. You are forever my King! Love you, talk to you soon." (4/25/16)

Latasha: "Love u back... I'm glad u are always there for me. U will always hold a place in my heart. We have a very special bond." (7/11/16)

Hope: "Hey Adore! How are you? I hope all is well. OK, I been researching a few things for starting your T-shirt business. I was wondering if you could design something around this pic I'm gonna attach? I would like to create a saying for being black, strong, and natural. It doesn't have to be the whole face or anything. Just let the pic inspire you... LOL. Let me just say, I know you're serious about this so that makes me super eager to get started too. Thanks... TTYL... Hope." (8/24/17)

Latasha: "Hey Boo. You are so silly. You know you are very special to me. We've always had a special bond. Never any pressure but we have so much respect for each other. We built that a long time ago. You always been about ur business. I can't wait till you get out because I know you will be great. You were born for greatness Boo. I really believe that. Love you for life." (2/16/18)

Dana: "Hey there, wow I looked you up to see if you was on Jpay. I didn't know if it would notify you... LOL wow its been years and that's sad on my part I should have done better, you were a very good friend to me." (4/12/18)

KeeKee: "Heyyyy boo, I miss you more, I'm jus maintaining working my butt off, trying to get this money for this deposit. I'm proud of you staying positive and focusing on doing your thing, jus wish u was here doing all that, I kno I can't rush time. I love you, till next time and here are some funny different faces of me being silly sitting on the toilet LMFAO, and no my shit don't stink." (4/27/18)

Shawna: "Snap n' Send(s)" (5/09/18)

Jasmine: "Good morning my King. I'm writing this as I'm on the phone with you my love LOL!" (5/18/19)

Salicia: "Great words of encouragement. I really appreciate them all. I love the positive energy and vibes, u almost made me shed a tear or two. I'm OK, I'm prepared for the worst and pray for the best. Whatever God says is what goes so I'm taking it one day at a time." (6/12/19)

Jon-Nika: "I just want to say I hope you can forgive me for the way things turned out. I do have a new number its." Etc. (7/10/19)

Jamika: "I'm laying here trying to fall asleep but I drank too much caffeine today! I wish I was laying here waiting for you to get out of the shower... and I'm laying under the covers in my birthday suit... you come over and pull on the sheets playfully as I fight you from taking a peak. If you want to see you will have to work for it... start with kissing my spot, my neck and then pin my hands behind my head so I can't move, this will drive me crazy and the juices will certainly flow. I need to be totally at your mercy. Take the sheets off forcefully, now softly suck and caress my breast as you move your hand down and feel my wetness flowing out.

I'm begging you to kiss her or rub her harder but you won't, you want me to explode before you enter me. I'm going crazy now because you won't even let me touch her, you continue to hold my hands and suck my breast. My hips are thrusting now because I can feel the head poking me and she wants him so badly. You stand over me and tell me I must 'earn that'... you place the tip on my lips and tell me to open wide. You begin to make love to my mouth... then you spread my legs and rub my clit as you go deeper and deeper inside of my honeypot with your fingers. You ask if I want you to kiss her and I beg you too... you then straddle me and place your penis in my mouth as you suck my clit, partaking in '69,' we cum together and lick up all of each other's juices.

That's round 1, you continue the story with round 2, I'm now about to rub her until I go to sleep. XOXO... Jamika." (8/01/19)

Jamika: "I go into the shower first. I'm shaving as you come in behind me and ask 'what are you doing to your girl?' I laugh and say, 'what does it look like Adore?' 'Didn't I tell you, she belongs to me in every way,' you quickly replied. You take the razor and meticulously begin to shave her so gently and smoothly. Watching you work is turning me on. Your skill with the razor matches that of the pen. You then take the showerhead down and rinse the soap off of me, using it to massage all over my body. The water pressure feels so good against my body. Taking your fingers and spreading my lips apart while the showerhead remained spraying on my clit, added to my climax. The water is powerful and almost too much for me to stand. I beg you to stop because she is becoming so tender. The more I beg, the more turned on you are getting. You stop and pull me closer to you. We kiss passionately and you gently push me down to your manhood. I begin to massage and suck him. I pay special attention to your balls, placing them in my mouth one at a time. This is driving you crazy. I keep sucking on them, as you stroke your penis up and down.

You stroke your penis faster and faster with the tip of the head beating against my soft wet lips. I keep my mouth and tongue open, I'm ready to receive all that you have to offer. You tighten up and I know he's ready for me now. I begin to suck his head as your proteins drip down my face and breast. Now you are begging me to stop sucking but I won't. You grab my head as you release the last of it and collapse against the shower wall. We sit together and let the water clean us up. Good night my King... XOXO." (8/06/19)

Diane: "Hiii how are you Adore? I'm good, at work right now driving. FYI your tattoos are a work of art. I wasn't trying to look too hard while you was with your visitor, didn't want to be rude. Idk if my brother told you a little about me but I'm cool peoples, just don't get on my bad side. I don't have a problem with giving my number out, I just work crazy hours getting my life back on track, etc., etc." (8/27/19)

Jasmin: "Snap 'n Send(s)" (9/16/20)

Dana: "Hey, so I set up a video visit for Saturday morning." (1/28/21)

Krystal: "Kisses." (5/19/21)

Salicia: "Oh my, how are u sweetheart? I know its been forever and I do apologize about that. I've had so much going on with myself here lately. So many setbacks just to be back at a good place. Sometimes I shut down and tend to separate myself from the world because I'm not exactly where I want to be so I try to stay focused. I never forgot about u." (8/12/21)

READ THIS ENTIRE BOOK
READ THIS ENTIRE BOOK
READ THIS ENTIRE BOOK
READ THIS ENTIRE
READ THIS ENTIRE
READ THIS ENTIRE BOOK
READ THIS ENTIRE BOOK
READ
READ THIS
READ THIS
READ THIS
GOD
LOVE
FREE
BOOK
BOOK
READ THIS ENTIRE BOOK
READ THIS ENTIRE BOOK
READ THIS ENTIRE BOOK

Again, I wasn't shy of having a plethora of "female friends." It wasn't until 10/08/21, when I received my first message through Meet-an-Inmate.com, from a sexy chocolate Queen from Atlanta Georgia. Not really sure what happened to "Tammy from Atlanta?" She sent one pic/message and disappeared?

Tammy: "Hi Adore, I came across your profile and was interested in being your friend. My name is Tammy. I'm from Atlanta Georgia and I'm 30." (10/08/21)

My next hit came from a super high energetic Spanish Queen from Houston Texas. Grace was cool, intelligent, bilingual, thick, sexy, etc. Grace's super high energy was a bit too much for My demeanor. However, I did try to plug her in with another brother incarcerated with me. It was a good match up.

Grace: "Hola Adore, first and foremost I want to say hello, happy holidays, God bless you, and nice to meet you. If you would like you can write me back, my address is... (etc.) God bless you and I look forward to hearing from you, kind regards." (12/5/2021)

Then came "Daisha from Indianapolis," very attractive, smart, hard-working mother of one son. Daisha's drip was crazy, and her beautiful skin complexion (coco brownish) added to her curvey natural figure. It didn't take long for both of us to figure out that our busy work schedules didn't coincide with each other's. Therefore, we both respectfully fell back... on a good note.

Daisha: "Hello love, hope your day was great. I accomplished absolutely nothing today=0(. So when y'all are short staffed y'all have to go on lockdown? I'm sending a few pics LOL, just know I be looking different with each look. Btw, I love the attachments you send=0)." (12/16/21)

Shortly after my born day in 2022, I received a message from "Marion."

Marion: "Hi Adore, hope you're having a good day! I came across your profile and you've got a cool vibe so I figured I'd reach out. My name is Marion, I'm 34 and I live in Silver Springs Maryland. I've never written anyone incarcerated, so not totally sure what all to put but I'll give it a shot!

I'm single, no kids, two pit bulls. Working on 2 master's currently, so school is pretty much my life these days. I'm originally from Philly, so I'm big on Philly sports but grew up mostly in Maryland.

Checked out your IG, you've got some cool artwork. Definitely creative! Not something I ever got good at LOL but my cousin is a graphic artist who does stuff for (etc.)

I could write a bunch of nonsense but I don't know how much you'd care about all that. If you're interested, write me back and I can go into more detail. Have a great day! Marion." (1/11/22)

Marion: "Morning! Dinner was good, thanks. Our old family dog is slowly dying so I try to go up at least once a week to visit & check on him.

Thanks, this is probably my favorite hair color. I've been almost every color of the rainbow & an actual rainbow at one point. I'm naturally a brunette but I've been blonde since I was 12 or 13, but I get bored being "normal" so I end up playing with colors. I take a lot of vitamins to keep my hair healthy. That's cool, I saw that on your profile. I'm sure you're popular in prison LOL everyone wants a haircut.

How did I find you... good question. I've known about writing inmates forever, but never thought about it. But I watch a TON of crime shows & documentaries and got more curious about the human aspect to it all, so I looked it up. You were actually one of the first names I came across.

Pitt bulls are a big passion of mine, diehard Eagles fan. I like cooking and baking, drinks, restaurants & trying new things, spending time with friends and family, traveling, music, hiking, and I love the beach. I love tattoos, always working on more artwork. What about you?" (1/13/22)

Marion received an "A +" in regards to making me feel like her extra school credits. My short communication lane with Marion felt like some type of "experiment." Marion acted as if she was secretly TRYING to find out any information from me, about being incarcerated as a Black Man, in "Virginia." Either way, I wasn't feeling her vibes at all. Thanks but no thanks, therefore, I respectfully fell back.

On February 9th, 2022, I received my first message from "Terria," residing in "Houston Texas."

Terria: "Hi Adore, a colleague of mine was showing me the website and how she met her guy she's been talking to. I seen your picture and felt like I just needed to get to know you but was a little shy. I just needed a little push I guess. Lol!

I'm 40 plus with no kids. I was born in Kansas City, but raised in Chicago. I'm currently residing in Houston, Texas. I been here since 2015, I have a MBA in (etc.) and work as an (etc.) I love to travel, spend QT with my family, have game nights and sometimes hangout with my girls. I workout and go to dance class just for cardio. Lol! So tell me about yourself Adore." (2/9/22)

The very next day, February 10th, 2022, I received a message from "Kadesha from North Carolina."

Kadesha: "Hey, my name is Kadesha. I'm interested in getting to know you, when you get some time give me a call." (2/10/22)

Kadesha also sent some pics of herself... Kadesha's super thick figure and super cute face made it easy for my eyes to stay focused on her southern thickness. However, Kadesha was only 19, too young for me. Therefore, we both respectfully fell back... on a good note.

My energy began to pull more towards Terria... after all, she's intelligent, independent, sexy, and thus far... she seems to have good vibes with positive energy. Who knows... Terria might be that special one???

Terria: "Hi Adore, I'm relieved to know there was a glitch with the computer and that's why I didn't receive a response until now from you. I was starting to think, maybe you weren't in to me. Lol! I seen your work on Instagram and I'm blown away by your work.

You sound like you have your head on straight and I really like that. I have no doubt that we can have deep intellectual conversations. This is a judge free zone. I had to look at the previous email I sent you and I forgot to mention that I'm married but we've been separated for almost a year now and it feels soooooo good. He was a serial cheater until he wasn't anymore, but when he was ready to change, I had already checked out the marriage mentally, so I moved out and just been focusing on myself, work, and my businesses.

Have you ever been to Houston? Are you close to your family? A few of my single girlfriends are celebrating valentines together so all isn't lost. Lol! I guess! I'm so happy that this will be a good valentines for you. Lol! I would like to continue to get to know you if that's alright with you. I have so much to ask and talk about but too much for one email so I'll get to it in each email I send to you.

Do you have kids? What's your favorite color? What type of movies you like? Do you have any siblings? Do you like pets? Have you ever been in a serious relationship? Hope to hear from you soon. To be continued." (2/11/22)

Finally, someone I can build with. Terria is smart, beautiful, super thick, hardworking... and she's really feel'n me. I will admit... Terria knocked me off of my feet, it wasn't long after that I began to have feelings for her that I had NEVER felt for any other woman prior to her. Is this real "love," only time will tell???

Terria: "Have you been getting my emails? I don't think so but I really hope you get this one. I attached some valentine pics for you. I really hope you like them cause this took me completely out my comfort zone. Lol! Will you be my valentines Adore? If so, happy valentines babe." (2/13/22)

Terria: "Good morning babe, its 8:21am and today I start my new position that I've been promoted to. Today will be a long day with learning a lot of new things that are needed for me to be successful in this new position. I woke up with you on mind and I wonder if you think of me too. Lol! I love your sense of humor and you seem pretty sure of yourself and true to who you are and I really like that about you. You are handsome and very intelligent with a high intellect that is a complete turn on for me.

I'm definitely very much into you and hope you feel the same about me. I can't wait to hear your voice in just live in that moment. Happy Valentines Day babe!" (2/14/22)

Terria: "My kids are getting older so they be doing their own thing. Lol! I'm saying all of this to say, you have my undivided attention Adore, and I mean that. I'm not a serial dater and never been. I'm a one man's woman. My soon to be ex husband was a serial cheater and had no romantic bones in his body. I know what I want and deserve out of a man. I want to be your peace not your worry. I want to be your escape from chaos. I want to get to know everything about you. I want you to know I'm not going anywhere and I'm here for you. To be honest, I'm still processing this whole thing. LOL!!! I can't wait to hear your voice. My nipples are getting hard just thinking about it. Lol! Sorry but its true. Lol!" (2/14/22)

Terria: "Hey babe, It was good to hear your voice. I felt like I've known you all my life. That's the vibe I was getting. Lol! I love your energy and can't wait to learn more about you. I can now picture us spending time together and just having a great time. Your drive and ambition is a complete turn on. Your confidence will knock down any wall that stands in your way. I can see it. God sure does has His hands on you. You're going to do great things Adore. I believe in you and your vision and it will definitely come into fruition.

Talking to you felt like a magnet pulling me closer to you. Lol! Sounds crazy but I don't know another way to explain it. Well I hope the stupid machine gets fixed so you can finally read my letters. Hope you are thinking of me like I'm thinking of you babe.

Sending you my love, kisses, and positive energy. To be continued...."

Terria: "Good afternoon my King. I'm sitting in my office thinking about you and all the things I want to do to you. I'm so horny right now and my pussy kat is so wet. I get like this sometimes just out the blue. Lol! I want to kiss down your chest and then take my tongue and lick your dick from the tip of the head and taste your pre-cum form. You are getting aroused by my teasing.

You taste so good so I use my tongue to help lift and guide your dick right into my mouth. You look up at me but it feels so good to you that you throw your head back into the pillow. You tell me to stop because you don't want to cum too soon. So I stop briefly (5 seconds) and continue sucking your dick with my tongue latched to licking the side and tip of your dick, while my head repeatedly moves up and down. Satisfying my King turns me on and makes me soak my panties. I'm going to stop right here and let you finish.

Lol! To be continued...."

Terria: "I met my ex when I was 20, he was my first boyfriend, first everything. So I've never been with anyone other than him. I'm a one man's woman. I'm not a serial dater. If we are together than we are together, no questions asked.

I just wanted you to know some background, (etc.) little by little, now digest it. Lol!

I'll be messaging you like this often babe. I have nothing to hide. I will lay everything out there. To be continued...." (2/16/22)

I will be the first to admit... I instantly fell in love with Terria. She swept me off of my feet with her charm, looks, and determination. I started to focus completely on her, us, and our futures together... for what I thought would be "forever." Therefore, my love for Terria cosigned me to ask "THE BIG QUESTION?"

Terria: "YEEEEEEEEEESSSS!!! I WILL MARRY YOU BABE!!! I can't believe God came down and touched us. He has given me someone I never knew I needed bae. Thank you God for this man that I'm willing to spend the rest of my life with, and in death. My heart is so full babe. Its running over with unconditional love for you babe. I'm going to make you so happy. I'm betting it all on you babe. Its running over with unconditional love for you babe. I'm going to make you happy. I'm betting it all on you my love. You are my King Adore, and I promise to always have your back no matter what. I promise to wait for you. I promise to be your biggest supporter and cheerleader. I promise to never give up on you. I will always be loyal to you and our goals. We will become a strong and solid blended family, God willing.

I'm really amazed by your drive babe. Don't ever lose that my love. With our drive and ambition, there's nothing we can't do. We will be the couple people envy. We will love hard. We will pray hard, but most of all we will love God harder, for it was He who put us together.

I can't wait til you come home babe. I know you're eager to get your career back started and I'll be there with you rooting you on, but until then, I will continue to hold it down here for the both of us. If I have it then you have it. I got you babe. We'll figure all this stuff out and roll with it.

I LOVE YOU MY SWEET LOVING HUSBAND,

MR. ADORE HSAAF.

To be continued...." (2/16/22)

Terria: "My King Hsaaf. Bae, I love talking to you. I feel like I can tell you any and everything. I love you for that. Damn babe, you came and scooped me up and made me a believer that real love still exist no matter where you at or what your circumstances are.

I love that you seem so sure of yourself, and what you want, and you stand on that. That's a complete turn on babe. Lordt! You're all mines bae! Yeeeeeeess! I'm super proud of the man you've become considering your circumstances babe. That shows real growth. I can't wait till the day comes where we can spend the rest of our lives together. Its me and you husband. If I gotta marry your ass in prison then that's what I'ma do. Lol! Fa Real!

I'm not going anywhere no matter what!

So babe have you ever been to Disney World? I've always wanted to but never been. I want us to go. I can't wait to meet your side of the family. I want them to witness the love I have for you, the love we have for each other.

My family will absolutely loooooove you. You would fit in like the perfect puzzle piece babe. My mom is a sweetheart. You'll see how close me, my mom, and siblings are. We all live no more than 15 minutes away from each other. Lol!

Babe, I want to give you evening rub downs and cook for you. So many things I have in store for my husband. You'll see.

Give me kisses bae." (2/16/22)

Terria: "Like I said before, if we have to get married while you're in prison then that's what I will prepare to do babe. I want to be your wife. Sending you all my love and kisses MR. HSAAF!" (2/16/22)

Terria: "My King MR. HSAAF, its 2/17/22, 5:21 AM. I'm up watching the news and thinking about my future husband. I hope you slept well, but I know you wont experience the perfect sleep until you're here next to me in our king size bed. Oh! And those kisses you sent me last night to place anywhere I wanted, got placed right here, here, oh, and right here too! Yeah, you know the places. Lol!

I'm still processing the fact that you are the first thing I think of in the morning and last before I lay my head down at night. I prayed to our Father God last night and had a conversation with him about us and our future. I felt more at ease this morning so I know he's listening and working on me, on us babe. We have nothing to worry about babe. My mind is made up! I want to and I'm going to be your FOREVER!

You will NEVER be alone here on out. I'm going to do life with you regardless of your situation.

YOUR WIFE FOREVER,

MRS. HSAAF" (2/17/22)

Terria: "Babe you are the fuckin MAN! I love how you carry yourself. Your confidence owns any room you're in because you know who you are as a person and people can feel that and therefore they will respect you. I love hearing your voice. I love how you talk to me. I can feel all your love and every word you say and/or write me. I know its real babe! I wouldn't change any of this for NOTHING! What we have is priceless." (2/17/22)

Terria: "Hey babe, I don't know why I be expecting your call all the time. I be checking my phone to make sure the volume is turned all the way up after I've just checked the volume like 5 minutes ago. Lol! Hilarious! I blame you babe! You must have put Voodoo on me or something. I tell ya, I ain't NEVER been this way for NOBODY! But somehow you were able to do it. But who's complaining? NOT ME! Lol! So yea, I'm about to go home and grab something to eat and watch a lil bit of Martin (the episode of his missing CD player) I'll be waiting for you to call home babe. Love you always, MRS. HSAAF." (2/17/22)

Damn... Terria actually told me on the phone to "take that profile down." Basically, she wants me to cancel my Meet-an-Inmate page. My mind was racing at posthaste speeds. "If I don't take it down she's probably going to think that I'm not serious about our marriage, but if I do take it down and she's not ready or changes her mind about getting married... then what?" I nervously thought to myself. I thought long and deep about it... and my final decision... I decided to have my Meet-an-Inmate profile removed. I figured it was the correct choice, after all... I had found my "MRS. RIGHT," and I felt great about my soon to be"Wife."

READ THIS ENTIRE BOOK
READ THIS ENTIRE BOOK
READ THIS ENTIRE BOOK
READ THIS ENTIRE
READ THIS ENTIRE BOOK
READ THIS ENTIRE BOOK
READ THIS ENTIRE BOOK
READ
READ THIS
READ THIS ENTIRE BOOK
READ THIS ENTIRE
THIS ENTIRE BOOK READ READ
READ THIS ENTIRE BOOK READ
THIS ENTIRE BOOK READ
GOD
LOVE
FREE

Terria: "My babe said " TAKE MY PROFILE DOWN ASAP." Yeeeessss! You put that urgency in that letter babe... letting them know this shit is time sensitive. That's what's up babe. You did a damn good job writing that letter babe. You are the SHIT! THAT'S MY MAN, MY HUSBAND, MY BABE, MY WORLD, MY EVERYTHING AND MORE... MY KING MR. HSAAF. I'm so proud to be your woman. I'm super proud to call you my man. ALL MIIIIIIIINES! I love you babe." (2/17/22)

Terria: "Baaaaaaaabe!!! Lol! I can't wait to give you all my lovin. I need you. I want you. I got you for life. I'm horny and I can only think about our brief nasty session on the phone. Hehehehehe! So I attached a couple pics so you can see what I'm in the mood for. Lawd! I can't wait to ride your dick and take it out to suck it and ride it some more. I want you to fuck me so good. I'm not worried cause I know you gon lay that dick on me. Now smack my ass babe.

I love you MR. HSAAF." (2/17/22)

Terria: "Hey King! Its always good to hear your sexy ass voice babe. I be smiling from ear to ear whenever I see you calling or even just thinking of you. The butterflies come full force every time. We're about to embark on a journey that we both prayed for and dreamt of. Babe, I deeply love and care for you like no other. WOOOOOOW!!! You put that good ole Voodoo on me babe. Lol! Fa real! I've been on cloud 9 all week. Our lives will forever change here on out my love. We're on our way up like the Jefferson's. Lol! Hehehehe!" (2/18/22)

Terria: "I've always wanted to be fucked in a kitchen. We both meet each other at home on our lunch break. You rushed forward hooking your left arm under my leg, and your right arm holding my waist, lifting me onto the counter. I bit my lips as you lowered your head to give my tight pussy a lick. You longed for it even more than I knew, you really do enjoy orally pleasuring your Queen, for a multitude of reasons, the taste, the texture, the aroma, the sound of my moans, groans, and the rhythmic twists and contortions of my body. Its like an aphrodisiac. You pulled my panties to one side and licked my sweet brown lips open to get at my pinkness below.

You acknowledged my groans as I arched my back and titled my hips, giving you more access to my most sensitive parts. You circled my clit then sucked it into your lips, stroking it with your tongue and returning to start again. Each repetition became more intense.

'Oh fuck,' I said impatiently. 'Quick, I need you inside me,' I demanded anxiously.

You savored the taste of my delicacy as I scooted off the kitchen counter and got on my knees. You said 'open wide,' my eyes lit up as I engulfed the end of your dick in my mouth. I sucked your dick hard and took it in as deep as I could without gagging. I spit and slurped on your dick as you let out a loud moan... 'daaaaaaamn Bae, suck it!' Your hands grabbed the back of my head as I sucked your dick harder. 'Now that's a good girl, ohhhh yes, a really good girl,' you whispered softly. Bent over with my dress pulled up, you took your long----thick erected dick and began to tease my pussy with it, sliding it with my juices all the way to my clit and back, teasing your tip against the opening of my pussy only to slide it back up to my clit again. I moaned... 'stop playing with me, awwfaaaak...'

Pushing your dick through my tight wet pussyhole, made my body stiffen and my stomach drop lower. You edged yourself deeper and I stood on my tip-toes with one hand on the counter and the other rubbing my wet pussy while you fucked me from the back. 'AHHHHHH SHIT DADDY! YAAAAASSSS, DON'T STOP BABE!' I blurted out impulsively. I assured you that your dick felt good inside of me. The look on your face confirmed that it was the best pleasurable moment of your life. Your sweat dripped from your face onto my lower back and down the crack of my ass.

'Fuuuck yeeees.' I squealed, 'faster... faster.' I quickly demanded. You complied with my demands as I repeated to you, 'don't stop.' The pitch in my voice got higher with each demand. Thrusting your hips into my ass cheeks hard, fast, and deeply, while pulling my hips back with every push, made my pussy contract firmly around your shaft. My words transformed into inaudible jibberish and my body turned to jelly.

My contractions also triggered you, as my pussy gripped your dick, you closed your eyes and started moaning uncontrollably. I knew exactly what was coming next, you... you pulled your dick out of my soaking wet pussy and I dropped to my knees, I let you explode in my mouth. I swallowed your soldiers and licked my lips at the end. You lifted me up and we both stared into each other's eyes with silence... we kissed and held on to each other as if our bodies were speaking its own language and we were onlookers.

To be continued.

I LOVE YOU BABE!" (2/19/22)

Terria: "I'm going to try and push this divorce as fast as possible, so I need you to really be sure that you believe I'm the one for you. I need you to be sure of your feelings for me. I love you so much that it scares the hell out of me babe. But I'm betting and risking it all on YOU, MY KING, MY BABE, MY FOREVER, MY WORLD, but most importantly, MY HUSBAND.

I LOVE YOU FOREVER IN THIS LIFE AND THE NEXT!

I'm ready to spend the rest of my life with you or die trying." (2/19/22)

Terria: "I hope my letter didn't sound negative cause that wasn't my intentions babe. I'm just clear on what it is I want and need (which is you) and now I see that you are too. That's settled. I'm gon be lusting over your sexy ass too. Trust and believe! My pussy knows she belongs to you cause she purrs every time I think of you.

She be like 'where's BIG DADDY,' and I'll pet her and reassure her that 'DADDY will be home soon to attend to you.' Once I tell her that, she goes back to sleep like a good girl, or, if she still continues to yearn for your attention, my handy dandy purple friend will satisfy her on your behalf/absence.

I can't wait to receive your works of art in the mail babe. I promise to be real careful babe. I will be able to touch something that you touched. I will cherish everything you've made so don't worry about that MY LOVE. You know what picture stood out to me the most on your IG page? Its the painting of the fishes, because of how you incorporated your logo to blend into the fish's scales.

Your talent is out of this world. I'm so so so so very proud of you babe. You have dreams, aspirations, goals, drive, and the will to accomplish any and everything. I strongly believe in you and just to hear you speak so highly of the people you love and respect let's me further know, I've made the right decision in choosing you. I'm going to invest in you, we're going to invest in each other. Its US OVER EVERYTHING (well besides God, but you get what I'm saying lol).

I'm going to call it a night or should I say morning and get me a little rest before its time to get your call.

I LOOOVE YOU BABE!

Sending you all my love, kisses, hugs and positive thoughts and energy." (2/20/22)

Terria: "Babe let me tell you something Mr. Smarty Pants, there's no way in hell I'll ever get tired of you. I love the fact that you will keep me on my toes. Your ass is like an energizer bunny that keeps going and going. Lol! I'm so excited for this journey, our journey. I couldn't have never pictured this, but God, He's so amazing!!! We will continue to give him our praise, love and attention. Babe I know I'm going to keep saying this over and over but you are the shit!

Lol! You are a MAN!!! MY MAN!!! D-MAN!!! You are everything." (2/20/22)

Terria: "My love, I'm just getting out the tub. I soaked my body in this coconut milk and coffee bean sea salt bath scrub. My body needed that. My skin feel so silky smooth babe. Lol!

I'm so excited for our future babe. I can't wait to start coming home to you. I look forward to cooking for you, nursing you when you are sick, rubbing your back and shoulders when you're feeling tense, pillow talking with you, and just being there for you the only way I know how.

Adore babe, I want you to know, I'm satisfied and content with what we have. I know your situation is temporary so I'm not thinking about what's in them streets. Please understand babe that I would never in a million years, disrespect you or our relationship/marriage. I've never out my 44 years of life, met anyone like you. You're everything I asked God for. And listen to this, when I prayed, I asked God to send someone in my life years from now when I thought I'd be ready to be in a serious relationship because I honestly thought I wasn't and I didn't want to be in any type of friendship/relationship with NO ONE! BUT BOOM!

God had other plans. Your ass came and showed out and changed my HEART. And you think I'll fuck that up for any kind of pleasure with someone besides my husband ADORE MF'N HSAAF?!?! If you ever have that thought in your head, you need to think again and check yourself at the door babe cause that's not gonna happen, NOT NOW, NOT EVER!!!

This is the best feeling in the world babe. You are my world now and there's no going back. DONE AND DONE!!!

Goodnight my love muffin. I LOVE YOU KING HSAAF." (2/21/22, 9:53PM)

Terria: "God brought you to me on a platinum platter." (2/23/22, 8:26AM)

Readers, have you ever heard the saying "love at first site"? Well in my case I fell in love at first type, Lol. I fell in love so fast that I didn't pay close attention to how Terria tried to fix all problems within a relationship, marriage, etc., with 'sex'. Every problem within a relationship can not be fixed by sex... physical sex or phone sex. In fact, anyone who tries to use sex to " fix" everything... is indeed showing signs of a "nymphomaniac," (Excessive sexual desire in and behavior by a female).

Terria: "Adore, Adore, Adore! The Love of my life. My everything. The man that makes me better. The man that loves and encourages me to be the best version of myself. The man that I know will go to the end of the world for me. Babe I'm sorry for fucking up our very first visit. I just can't believe I didn't take the time zones in consideration. I'll make it up to you Daddy. I promise babe.

Sooner or later we won't have to deal with this shit. You'll be home with your family waiting for you with open arms and hearts. I will catch your ass off guard a lot. You'll be on the phone or painting/drawing, watching sports, etc., and I'll come out with something real sexy on, smelling all good, have some sexy ass pantyhose on for you to rip off my bare ass. I just made you forget what it was you were doing. I'll tie your hands behind your back so you won't be able to touch the GOODS, LOL! I'll have on my black stilettos, standing in front of you. I'll turn around with my ass poked out, and bend over in front you with my crotchless pantyhose on so you can see how wet my pussy is. You're unable to touch me due to your hands being tied behind your back.

I can see how much you are turned on by it because your dick is standing at attention. I take your boxers off so I can see how swollen and stiff your dick is. There's pre-cum dripping from the side of your dick and I kneel down to lick it, and all you can say is 'daaaaaamn babe, that shit feels good, now suck my dick.' You demanded, but I pretended I didn't hear you and I continue to tease you. Its torture for you because now I've climbed on top of you and I start to rub my tight pink pussy on the head of your stiff dick.

You try to grab my nipple with your tongue but I jerk back so you can't. You're like 'baaaaabe, stop this shit and untie me NOW!' You're ready to fuck me like you've never fucked me before. I untied you and you flipped me on my back and rammed your stiff dick inside me, and I let out the loudest gasp.

It feels so good and I'm telling you to 'FUCK ME BABE, YES! JUST LIKE THAT DADDY! RIGHT THERE BABE THAT DICK IS SO GOOD!' You're going crazy in my pussy and we both cum at the same time, my legs give out. I'm left with no energy. Lol!

I will NEVER do you wrong. NEVER! When I'm not on the phone with you, I keep your voice in my head telling me something sweet and I'm smiling ear to ear babe. It happens every time. You never in your life have to be alone babe. I'm ready to go through the mud with you babe. Sending you all my love, kisses, hugs, and positive energy." (2/24/22)

Terria: "My Loving Husband, now, as far as me letting the people closest to me know about you, I've told a couple people (mom, one of my sisters, my best friend) and plan to tell others as we go. I need you to understand something, I'm very protective of you and what we have. Not everyone will understand what we have, and therefore, I'd rather let them know about you once you come home.

I don't need nor want the negativity. You have to understand that I'm in the middle of a divorce, so I don't want to give my ex NOOOOOO ammunition to use against me in any court hearings if I tell the wrong person about you. Trust and believe bae, I can't wait to shout your FUCKING NAME to the world! I am so very proud of my KING! And everybody will know and see that about you when that time comes.

I have to navigate this very strategically, to make sure you are announced and represented in the best way possible. I love you babe and can't wait to spend the rest of my life with you. That's all I want. Please just bare with me." (2/25/22, 10:34AM)

Terria: "MY EVERYTHING AND FOREVER! Babe it was a real joy seeing my husband for the very first time. My heart felt so warmed and the butterflies stayed in my stomach during the entire video visit. Lol! It felt so surreal babe. Each day my love grows stronger for you but TODAY my love grew times ten. Hehehehehe! I wanted to jump through that damn screen so bad, hug and kiss you until we both get tired.

MR. ADORE MF'N HSAAF! MY KING, MY WORLD, MY COMFORT, MY PEACE, MY PAIN IN THE ASS, MY HUSBAND! I love how you carry yourself. Your cocky ass is a complete turn on and you know it but I love it. Lol! I never want you to change who you are for NO ONE! You've created a lane that no one else could create if they wanted to. You are a true leader of the people and a student for GOD. I FUCKIN LOVE YOU BOY! That's my babe.

Babe your lips are so juicy and just... Damn! I just want to suck on them. I gotta go cause I'm driving myself crazy, shit got damn. Lol! I LOVE YOU HUSBAND!!! Best believe I'm not playing behind you."

(2/25/22, 4:18PM)

Terria: "Babe, Let me say this, my ex was very insecure and controlling and manipulative. Once upon a time, after I had given birth to my child in 2008, I got really sick. I use to pass out all the time and had to get constant blood transfusions. The medicine I was on made me gain a lot of weight, etc. The whole time I was down and sick, that dude would come home, get cleaned up, and hit the streets. He thought if he was bringing in the money that I shouldn't have anything to say. Don't get me wrong, he never been physically abusive... well except for one time when he almost choked me to death after I told him I didn't want to be with him.

Let me tell you what this idiot did, one day he introduced me to his (then) best friend and his fiancée. My ex was supposed to be his best friend's best man in his wedding. We all went bowling together and had a good time.

One day I kept getting this bad feeling and I knew my inner intuition wasn't wrong, so one morning I picked up his phone and BOOM! There's hundreds of text messages to his best friend's fiancée. The very same fiancée he introduced me to. WOW!!! I really blanked out at this point but my mom told me I had hit him in the head with a trophy and left to go to class like nothing never happened. He was in the bed sleep when I had did this.

When I got done with class and went home and asked my mom why is there blood in my bed? What the heck happened? She told me what I had done. I thought her ass was crazy cause I told her 'I don't remember that.' My mom lived with us at the time.

Then maybe a week or two later I seen his ex best friend at a restaurant and he came up to me and told me that he had 'planned to kidnap' me, and beat me until I was unconscious just to get back at him, but he liked me and I didn't deserve that.

So look, I don't care what that nigga would agree or disagree with. I never deserved any of the shit he put me through. Adore, I've been faithful and loyal til the very end so I don't owe that nigga shit!!! Straight up!!!

Period!!! I don't want to talk about that bitch ass nigga NO MO!!!" (2/25/22)

Okaaaaaaay... now that was very unexpected, that message really threw my equilibrium completely off. Does she have any kids or not? The saying goes "there's two sides to every story." Thus far, I've yet to hear her ex's side, which basically leaves only her side of events. I must admit, I'm not a fan of one-sided stories. Regardless of Terria's prior "baby daddy" dramatized events, I still TRIED my very best to love her unconditionally, PERIOD.

Terria: "MY KING, I just got off the phone with you and from the first time we talked today, the energy was crazy off. I won't do the blame game but I promise to put the work in (on my end) to make our relationship last forever. I will never undermine you and dismiss your feelings.

I respect how you feel and I heard you loud and clear, so I will take heed to what you've said and plan accordingly. You're right, I'm out here and you're in there, so the most simplest forms of communication that we have access to in the outside world comes much harder for you behind those prison walls.

I know better and will do better here on out. I want to be your peace, and your temporary escape babe.

I'm not perfect and I might not always get it right all the time, but just know all I want is the best for you even if we don't survive as a couple. And I say that because I'm not sure where your head is and if by me not answering the phone was enough for you to give up on what we have.

You sounded so hurt and disappointed by me and I never want to make you feel like that. I can't stop crying right now and I'm feeling like this is a bad break up or something. Like for you to say you'll talk to me on Monday, I can't help but think you might be giving me bad news Monday morning.

I mean... I just love you so much babe. I'm going to end this letter cause the more I type, the more the tears roll from my eyes. Goodnight babe." (2/26/22)

That would be the first (but not last) time that I felt the negative cheating vibes from Terria. Her fake energies made it easy to see straight through her lies. Terria, began to shorten her own rope, she started to destroy her own trust.

Terria: "MY WORLD, you make me feel like I could do anything my love. I need you, I want you and can't do without you.

Mom and I had a long talk about you, us, and our future. She told me she couldn't wait to get me by myself to have this talk. She also requested to talk to you as well. I told her I would talk to you about it.

She said you've paid your debt to society and there will be no ill will or negative energy, she would never cast on you or our relationship. So please don't doubt for one second that I'm not serious about you or us. I'm preparing but in my own way. I told you to let me handle things here and I promise I will.

I will never in my life turn my back on you babe. No matter how mad or angry we might be at each other. I'm in this forever. Are you? Babe you never have to worry about me getting tired of you. I looooove seeing that number pop up on my phone. I know once I've heard your voice, my day is complete. I can actually go on with my day.

You do it for me babe! That's it! I'm all yours. You deserve the world, respect and honesty my love and I promise to give that to you or die trying.

I miss you babe!" (2/27/22, 7:54AM)

Terria: "Hey babe, in regards to your letter about having a 3some, no, I have not ever experienced a 3some before, but I would like to, with you of course. I've been approached by women several times. Just a matter of fact, I was approached by 2 different women almost 3 weeks ago at this lounge that me and (etc.) went to. Even the model that I'm in the photoshoot with even tried shooting her shot. Its crazy and I don't know what it is that makes them think I stroll that way? But I had to tell her that's not my thing and she was really surprised.

And babe let me just say this, I get asked out a lot and yes some at work too, but listen, I don't entertain that shit. These dudes be trying to impress you with material shit, cars, money, and what they can do for you. Lol! Shit is hilarious cause as soon as I tell them I can do all that shit for myself they be looking crazy. Lol!

Also, there's no comparison when it comes to you and my ex. Believe me, if you reminded me of him, I would've been blocked your ass. Lol! Trust! I'm not holding on to nothing in my past. When we first separated, I started seeing a Therapist for an entire year. It was one of the best decisions I've ever made besides leaving him.

I have a life coach that I've been seeing via Skype twice a month. I have a session with her tomorrow at 10:00AM. I LOVE YOU." (2/27/22, 10:02AM)

At this point, is it safe to say that Terria has made it very clear that she is NOT "bisexual"?

Terria: "Babe you got a hold on me. Do you know that? Lol! You are my King babe. My King! I'm just getting out the shower and I had 2 glasses of champagne. I'm so fuckin horny babe.

I have a T-shirt with no panties on. My pussy is wet and I haven't even touched it. The thought of my King's hands caressing my body is making my clit so hard and sensitive to the touch. I'm so horny, I don't even need the purple helper. Once I give it a couple of rubs I'll then have a much needed orgasm.

Laying next to you, just to turn over and see this fine ass specimen of a fuckin man. I can't help myself. My pussy knows your touch, your smell, and she can't help but to get overly excited and super wet. She's waiting for her King to play and fuck her real good.

I have a bunny tail butt plug to make it less painful to fuck me in the ass." (3/1/22, 10:48PM)

Terria: "Adore, I was molested by my mom's brother. I was (etc.) years old. I still remember what I had on and how my mom combed my hair. I had this beautiful deep red floral sundress on and I had two long pigtails with one blue and one red ribbon tied on each pigtail. I had big cheeks and a huge smile all the time. One day this PIG came to visit, my mom and dad asked him to watch me while they go pick up my siblings.

He told me to come in the bathroom and he started telling me how I was so pretty with a nice ass, he stood on top of the toilet seat and told me to open my mouth wide until he ejaculated in my mouth and had me to rinse my mouth, etc.

So when I was about (etc.) he had died. I was sooooo happy. I hated his ass. When mom asked me if I wanted to go to the funeral. I told her HELL NO!!!

That's exactly how it came out and she said, 'what did you say?' I changed it up and said 'no ma'am,' but til this day I wonder why she never asked me why did I react like that when she asked me did I want to go to the funeral. I was so mad at her because EVERYONE always put me on this high ass pedestal, I felt like I always had to be perfect. So I didn't want to disappoint my parents so I kept my mouth shut and continued to be that perfect daughter to them. When you meet my family, you will always hear my siblings say I'm my mom's favorite or I'm the family's best child. My aunts, uncles, and cousins will all tell you the same thing. Well at least until I started not giving a FUCK! I've cut off many people in my life. Mostly family.

That's why it was soooooo important for me to leave that marriage. It was always about him and never about me. It was the worst. It was mental abuse for SUUUUURE! NEVER AGAIN! So that's why getting a divorce was so important to me when I first filed last month. I need this for me because its loose ends, baggage, a fucking disease that I'm ready to get rid of forever.

And listen, when my ex and I got married, I refused to change my last name. I didn't start wearing that stupid wedding ring until (the year of) and we got married in (the year of). So yea, there's some of my truths for ya." (3/3/22, 1:40PM)

After reading that message, I was momentarily speechless, and confused, literally???

Terria: "We passionately kiss each other on the floor, I slightly sat on top of you. Your dick is roc hard... I started to roll my pussy on the tip of your dick. You want to stick it in my phat wet pussy kat but I won't let you. 'Come on babe, give daddy his pussy,' you said. Not until I land sweet kisses around your dick head. I start to lick the side of your dick with no hands or teeth, just my tongue and lips, smothering my DICK (cause that's mine) my babe moaning and telling me to 'take all that dick,' in my mouth (I gotcha babe) I do just that.

I started kissing your ankles all the way up to your neck... then I started nibbling and licking your neck while stroking your dick at the same time. As I'm laying on my back, you bend my legs back as far as they could go, and you start fucking me like you've never fucked me before.

THAT'S MY SPOT BABE, DON'T STOP FUCKING ME! I'M BOUT TO CUM BABE! Aah-----Ah... Y-yeeeesssss, DAMN! Babe that was good, you have some good dick babe. I love you my husband. Goodnight luv bug." (3/3/22, 11:03PM)

Terria: "MY EVERYTHING, I'M STILL AT WORK AND TYPING YOU BEFORE I LEAVE. I HAVE SO MANY EMOTIONS BABE (ALL GOOD). I SWEAR YOUR SMILE MELTS MY HEART BABE. I LOVE YOU SO MUCH MY LOVE. I'M DEDICATED TO YOU MR. ADORE HSAAF. LOL! NOT ONLY AM I DEDICATED TO YOU BY GETTING YOU HOME SOONER, BUT I'M ALSO DEDICATED TO FALLING INLINE WITH GETTING OUR BUSINESS AFFAIRS IN ORDER, GETTING THIS DIVORCE FINALIZED, AND MANY OTHER THINGS BABE.

PLEASE KNOW THAT I'M BEING PULLED EVERY WHICH WAY AND I HEARD YOU LOUD AND CLEAR. I NEED TO FIGURE OUT WHAT AND WHO SERVES A PURPOSE IN OUR LIFE/BUSINESS AND CUT OFF THE PEOPLE THAT DON'T. I WILL BE MAKING THESE CHANGES EFFECTIVE NOW. I WANT US TO BE ON THE SAME PAGE WITH EVERYTHING. AS LONG AS WE'RE LISTENING AND RESPECTING EACH OTHER, I KNOW WE WILL EVENTUALLY GET THERE BABE. I RECEIVED YOUR LONG ASS LETTER BABE AND WILL READ IT SOON. I CAN'T WAIT TO HEAR FROM YOU.

I LOOOOOVE YOU BOI!" (3/4/22, 5:04PM)

READ THIS ENTIRE BOOK
READ THIS ENTIRE BOOK
READ THIS ENTIRE BOOK
READ THIS ENTIRE
READ THIS ENTIRE
READ THIS ENTIRE BOOK
READ THIS ENTIRE BOOK
READ
READ THIS
READ THIS ENTIRE
READ THIS
GOD
LOVE
PEACE
FREE
BOOK
BOOK
THIS ENTIRE BOOK READ
READ THIS ENTIRE BOOK READ
THIS ENTIRE BOOK READ

In regards to the "affection," and "phone sex," Terria landed a "bullseye." However, there's more to a friendship, marriage, etc., besides "affection" and good "phone sex." In fact, I even appreciated Terria's financial support periodically. There's an old saying that goes, "what you eat don't make me shit." Basically, its good to know that Terria worked hard to take care of her household, bills, etc., but I also needed Terria to understand respectfully, that my current incarceration did not negate myself from also being a hard and dedicated worker with positive and strong work ethics.

Terria gave me her greenlight that she would fall "INLINE WITH GETTING OUR BUSINESS AFFAIRS IN ORDER." I took Terria's words as her personal bond, was I wrong for that? Either way, I couldn't stop doing what GOD Blessed me to do. WORK SUPER HARD AT ACCOMPLISHING ANYTHING I FEEL IS WORTH ACHIEVING POSITIVELY, PERIOD!

Terria: "I ordered Chinese food again and some alcohol and had Door Dash to deliver it. So I think I'm tipsy bae. I attached some pictures with this letter. I love our deep conversations and love sessions, because it erases doubts as well as some of the sexual tension. And let me let you in on a little secret. I've been sooooo satisfied after I've had an orgasm. Let me be more transparent with you, ADORE HSAAF, I'm the most happiest I've been in years." (3/4/22, 9:24PM)

Terria's unorthodox patterns of missed phone calls started to enhance rapidly, along with her fake excuses in regards to why she wasn't able to answer her phone. Being HONEST is a key element within any relationship, friendship, marriage, etc. The contrary of being honest is dishonest. Dishonesty is usually the foundation for someone who is labeled as being "fake." The contrary of "real," is "fake."

Terria's patterns of being fake didn't start when she met me, nor did her lies, these are all patterns of negative energies that she possessed waaaay before she reached out to me, through Meet-an-Inmate.com. I fell in love with a COMPULSIVE LIAR, FACT!

Introducing... TERRIA'S THROW OFF:

Terria's throw off consist of meticulous lies, made up to TRY and THROW a person OFF from THE PROBLEM(S) AT HAND. These lies are formulated by Terria with hopes to make you lose focus and "feel sorry," for her.

Example: Let's say I respectfully ask Terria why did it take her all day to answer her phone? Instead of Terria just being honest and stating the facts, after she makes a solid point of view, she will continue her lie by adding more frivolous poppycock, like....

Terria: "When I saw your missed calls, I jumped up, brushed my teeth and washed my face, walked the dog, came back in and threw some clothes on so I could go meet B in etc., which is 45 minutes from me, just to pick up some cash to borrow to fill my tank and pick up a few things I needed from the store.

B's best friend lives in etc., where there's nothing but freaking woods. So I don't know if you were calling me back then, but I didn't hear my phone ring until I just spoke to you.

Listen, you've explained to me the difficulties of having to plan to use the phone and I'm sorry I was unable to answer. So if you feel like you want to fall back from the phone then do that. If that's what makes you happy then by all means DO IT!!! Its not like I have any control in your decision RIGHT?!

We just had this same fallout last weekend and its draining because I don't want to spend my days upset at you or feeling like I can't be what you want all the time. We have so much to do and things like this only slows the process, so the ball is in your court. I'll let you do what you want with it.

BOOOOOOOY I'M SO FUCK'N PISS WITH YOU AND THIS PERON YOUR ASS TURNED INTO WHEN I MISS YOUR CALLS!!!!!!

I'm sorry Adore. That wasn't my intentions to be disrespectful. I knew if we were on the phone, you probably wouldn't have let me get a word in before going off. So I put it in the text. If you were here, there's no way I would have yelled at you cause I don't argue!

Let me tell you one more secret Adore. I had my child in 2009, and at that time I was diagnosed with postpartum depression. I was soooooo overwhelmed with life that I crushed up an entire bottle of sleeping pills and took them. My cousin Tory found me unresponsive in my bedroom, laying across my chassis. He gave me CPR until the paramedics came and pumped my stomach." (3/6/22)

Terria: "I didn't mean a lot of the stupid shit I said. I want to and I will break that wall that I've built. I will do better starting now. I'm not perfect but I know I will do all I can to make what we have work because you are worth fighting for. I LOVE YOU BABE." (3/7/22)

Terria: "There's no way you should be feeling the way you're feeling and just to know I was the cause makes me extremely sad. I AM SOOOOO SORRY! I LOVE YOU A. HSAAF!" (3/7/22)

Terria: "Peace King, to know you is to love you. You make me so very proud. You are so driven and ambitious and I absolutely looooove that about you, so please never lose that. You are a great teacher/leader and you make it look so easy, but we both know that's not true.

I brought a planner to start writing down goals/priorities. This will help us both (especially me) with the opportunity to see what's been done and what needs to be done. I realized I need to manage my time better. So starting tomorrow, we will discuss further. I'm ready for you and all that you bring.

Our session last night was amazing, and especially parking inside the restaurant's lot rubbing my pussy til I exploded on myself. Hearing your sexy ass voice gave me chills. You telling me how you want me and how you're going to eat my pussy, had me super wet. I had imagined sucking your dick while the spit drip down the sides of your dick and then BOOM! I had an orgasm just like that. I LOVE YOU MY KING." (3/9/22, 4:41AM)

Terria: "Babe, I'm sorry about that my love. My phone was plugged to the charger, at least I thought it was but the plug in the wall wasn't all the way plugged into the wall so my phone died.

Listen, don't be tripping on me neither babe when we talk. I hope I'm able to talk to you before the night is over." (3/12/22, 7:15PM)

Terria: "Now listen, I'm not gonna lie to you, but in the past I was definitely known for not answering my phone on purpose, but that's only if I was in a bad mood or just didn't want to be bothered, but I would NEVER not answer on purpose when you're calling me babe. That's insane. I loooove our conversations and I get super excited when I see you calling. But you know what? After thinking about it, I was like, if the shoe was on the other foot, I'd definitely feel the same way you be feeling. So that's a battle I know I'm not gonna win, so all I can do is try fixing this situation. Okay?" (3/12/22, 10:12PM)

Terria: "Hey, I tried answering the phone while in the movies. The movie started at 6:50 and its over at 10:05PM." (3/13/22, 7:06PM)

Terria: "Good morning my love, today should be a great day for the both of us. Why? Today marks our one month anniversary. One month of love, truth, tough conversation, arguments and lots of laughs. I didn't receive a call from you yet, so the first thing I'm guessing is that you took me off the phone list. I wouldn't be surprised.

I guess you checked out. I don't know... but what I do know is that I hold no grudges or ill will. That's not who I am as a person. I'm a good person that loves hard. I fight for the ones I love. I won't write much because I'm not sure if you would even read it.

Lord, I pray for unity in our relationship. Bind our hearts together, and may we be one as you intend for us to be. Help myself and Adore to honor and respect each other as the servant/leaders that you have called us to be, and teach us to love one another sacrificially as Christ loves the church (Ephesians 5:25).

Help us to have healthy communication and to speak words that will build us up and not tear one another down. Thank you Lord, that we can achieve unity and oneness through you. Amen." (3/14/22, 8:27AM)

Terria: "I haven't received any letters from you since 3/11/22, and I remember yesterday you telling me the kiosk was back up so I guess you probably X me out your life altogether then. This is super heartbreaking for me but if that's what you really want then I guess it is what it is.

I wish you all the happiness in the world Adore, because you deserve it and I know once you get out you are going to give everyone a run for their money. That's how talented and creative you are. No love will ever be lost. Love you always King. I'm deleting this app cause now there's no use for it. Take care Adore."

INSTITUTIONAL LOCKDOWN: Institutional Lockdown, is a period within the prison systems when the guards (Correctional Officers) and other "Staff" members, all come together and work extra hard to make Our (the Inmates) lives more miserable, LOL, somewhat... but not really. However, it is a period when we (the Inmates) have to lockdown in the cells (or dorms) and wait patiently for correctional officers to come in and rearrange our personal property, mail, food items, etc., looking for any "contraband" or any other objects that they can destroy or write charges for.

This process could sometimes take up to five or more days. An "institutional lockdown," is exactly what I was on during part of March, 2022, this is also the same timeframe Terria decided to set up a fake Jpay account. For some unknown realistic reason(s) within her own mind, she thought that she could "trick" me into believing that "Jessica" was just some random female that had viewed my profile on Meet-an-Inmate.com. Terria's immature games only deducted more of my trust from her... and her elementary writing skills quickly alerted me that "Jessica" was really "Terria." No sweat though, I'll play along with her little games... at least for now, LOL!

Jessica: "Hello Adore. My name is Jessica and after seeing your picture I wanted to introduce myself. I would love to get to know you better. So let me tell you a little about myself. I'm from Jackson Mississippi, but now live in Houston, Texas. I love to ride bikes, fish, read, shop etc. I'm a easy going person that live a quiet life in the Woodlands. Its a beautiful area to raise kids or just live. I would love to get to know you." (3/14/22)

Terria: "Believe it or not babe, we're still in the beginning stages of this relationship, and we're still learning each other. You're teaching me how to treat you and I'm only teaching you how to treat me. We have to be in uncomfortable spaces but that will pass but until it do, we need to have each others back, front and side.

Don't ever feel like you can't call me. I'm truly sorry for making you feel that way. I just want us to feel comfortable to be able to talk about anything. If I'm out of line, then tell me in that moment. But what makes me so angry with you is how you talk to me when you disagree with me. You talk at me as if I'm a child and I don't like that babe. I'm your woman, your Queen, your wife.

I LOVE YOU KING!" (3/14/22, 2:43PM)

Terria: "Hey babe, I know you told me if I don't hear from you in a few days then most likely you are on lockdown, but I still had to call to make sure and they confirmed that you are indeed on lockdown." (3/16/22, 8:10pm)

Jessica: "Hello there, how are you? I have not gotten a response from you so I hope everything is good on your end. I hope to hear from you soon." (3/21/22, 12:33AM)

Terria: "Listen, I had to do it. I needed to see how loyal you were. So now I believe what some people was trying to get me to see, which was, majority, if not all inmates are scheming ass niggas that will feed you jail talk. So now I'm convinced that they all were right. You fed me that jail talk bullshit. Everything was a LIE! I hope fuck'n over me made your nuts bigger.

So I'm giving your ass back to the streets. Them rusty, dusty ass hos can have you. Hopefully you'll find someone that's gonna be 10 toes down for you like I was. GOOD LUCK WITH THAT!!!! KING MY ASS!!!! MORE LIKE KING OF BEING THE BIGGEST FUCK'N ASSHOLE I KNOW!!!! So just in case you don't know what the fuck I'm talking about here you go playa. (3/23/22, 12:21PM)

Adore: 'Hello, I just viewed your name on my email account.'

Adore: 'Hi Jessica, how are you doing? What is it exactly that you would like to know about me? If possible, can you send some pics of yourself, so that I may also have a visual in regards to whom I'm communicating with?'

Adore: 'We have been on lockdown since 3/15/22, first chance I get I'll send this to you.' (3/17/22)

Adore: '(Sat) Still on lockdown, I'll send this to you ASAP.' " (3/19/22, 11:42AM)

THE PUPPET MASTER ROLE: The Puppet Master Role, is basically someone who controls the determined behavior of others, the "puppet," would be the actual person being mentally controlled. In this case, Terria thinks in her mind that she is the puppet master, and I am suppose to be the relationship's puppet. NOT! Terria doesn't want to see me happy with any other female(s) if it isn't "Terria."

Therefore, Terria will go above and beyond to push as much negative energy as possible towards interrupting any of my communication lanes, via Meet-an-Inmate.com. Terria's constant lies and disrespect set the foundation for a second chance at "true love," in other words... I made the moves to have my profile set back up, unbeknown to Terria... for now....

PROVERBS, C22 V 12 {"The LORD sees to it that truth is kept safe by disapproving the words of liars."}

READ THIS ENTIRE BOOK
READ THIS ENTIRE BOOK
READ THIS ENTIRE BOOK
READ THIS ENTIRE
READ THIS ENTIRE
THIS ENTIRE
READ THIS ENTIRE BOOK
READ
READ THIS
READ THIS ENTIRE
READ THIS
GOD
LOVE
BOOK
FREE
OOK
THIS ENTIRE BOOK READ
READ THIS ENTIRE BOOK READ
THIS ENTIRE BOOK READ

Not long after my profile was back up, a beautiful and smart Black Queen from Georgia, reached out to me. "Nika," check her out....

Nika: "Hello, I hope everything is going ok for you. I guess I will jump right into answering your questions. Well... I'm 30, live in GA, no kids, no pets. I'm an entrepreneur, have been since 2014, never believed in working for anyone. I definitely hated working jobs. Right now I'm actually building up a nonprofit that provides clothing for children, and I day trade. In between time I design candles and things like party accessories & clothing.

As far as something interesting about myself, that would depend on what type of things you find interesting. I just know I'm not a boring person! Love to take risks when it comes to my career & never afraid to step out on faith if its something I really want to do. This might be interesting, I'm on a 7 day smoothie diet. This is day 3! I hope I covered all your questions and some!

Your wording is very formal. Is that you as a person in general or just how you write? Where are you from? Age? Previous occupation? Life goals? Religious? If I'm not intruding too much, why are you incarcerated? Have a release date?

Sent a pic! Its literally my most recent pic so I decided to send it. Talk to you soon!" (3/31/22)

Meanwhile Terria wants to have her cake, ice cream, and personalized napkins with her initials on them, etc. Terria is

TRYING TO RUN HER BEST GAME ON ME. Terria's crux strengths consist of TRYING to puppet master me during my incarceration, while simultaneously fucking off with other people within society.

Basically, Terria wants my sincere love, affection, knowledge, and anything else that she can gain from my mental. However, whenever she feels the urge to "fuck," that's exactly what she's going to do. PERIOD.

Terria: "Peace King, Adore babe, I love you so got damn much. You are my puzzle piece I've been needing and wanting. You came in my life just when I had given up on love. I didn't want NOTHING to do with it. Babe all I want to do is love you and love on you. Like damn! I'm crazy about you ADORE HSAAF."

(4/1/22, 8:45AM)

What a way to start off "April fools day." Lol! Meanwhile, I was really starting to feel Nika's positive vibes, and vice versa.

Nika: "Hello. I believe you probably do get a lot of crazy people hitting you up daily. I have nothing against gay people either. My gay cousin lives with me until she finds her a new place. However they do tend to go after heterosexual people, especially the gay men. Its crazy. But I feel you!

So I assume you're not going to answer any of my questions. Since the ball is back in my court, I thought I'd let you know that you're such a bad sport! You've literally responded to me like 2-3 times since then and not answered one question. How are you going to say I can ask you 'whatever,' but then you proceed to give me somewhat of an ultimatum, then ignore every single question I asked? How am I suppose to get to know you? I only asked basic shit anyways. You prefer answering over a phone call? Because we can have a whole interview phone call. Lol. You'd probably be ready to hang up on me. But I must warn you, that I am country. So do not pick on how I talk.

I showed my best friend a portion of one of your messages. She was like 'oh y'all are going to bump heads a lot'. I'm an alpha female, very strong willed, somewhat spoiled, and I love to have my way. But I do work hard for myself. I'm still in bed being lazy. Didn't feel like getting up and making myself presentable for a pic to send. So I snapped a selfie... and yes I still have my bonnet on. Don't talk about me. Lol. I'm as upfront as it can get.

OK... so I caught the hint at the end of your last message. I assume it was a hint seeing you, talking to you, so here's my number (etc.) You can call tomorrow (Tuesday) between 11am-2PM, or today around 6P, if you get this in time. Its 4:20P now, so idk if you'll get it before then or not. I will ttyl." (4/4/22)

Terria: "You might be wondering if I've been with a woman, the answer is NO. I've been asked out by women, I've even flirted with women, but never have I ever been with another women. But see, the question you should be asking is if I would like to have a sexual encounter with a woman? I do. It would never be with someone I'm really cool with. Some of the women I hang with are either married and going through the same thing I was going through with my ex, and some are single. Its so much I want to do babe. I have no problem sharing any of my life with you but I need you to understand, I'm literally a late bloomer, Lol! I know it may be hard for you to believe but I am. I never had morning sex, EVER!

Its so much I want to explore with you. When you tell me to keep it real with you, I literally don't understand what it is you want from me or trying to get out of me. To really be honest with you, I'm somewhat embarrassed because I feel like I let my whole life just pass me up without really living. Adore, I am not your average woman. I have several fantasies, I would love to experience public sex, water sex, and all the different types of sex there is. Lol! I want to only experience this new life journey with you Adore. Babe, I really have it bad for you. Lol!

I love the idea of having a few sexy beautiful women with me... and we dance for you as we strip naked. You have your boxers on, and your hands are tied behind the chair. Your roc hard dick turns me and the other women on to the max. You want to touch so bad but you can't. We're all dancing and shaking our asses all in your face... we even start touching and kissing each other as you watch.

Your boxers are getting wet with pre-cum, so I signal one of the women to start sucking your dick and then I join her. The other two women come over and lay on the floor... waiting for me and the other girl who's sucking your dick to sit our sweet wet pussies on their tongues. Now, I want you to watch these 3 women lick on, suck on, and fuck on your wife. I'm sitting on one's face while she eats my pussy, the other is eating my ass and the other is sucking my titties. Watching your wife get pleased by 3 beautiful women, is a sight for you to see.

I look you in your eyes and ask you, 'like what you see babe, huh, you like how she's eating your wife's pussy?' You quickly replied, 'YEEEES BABE YEEEES!' My pussy is dripping wet and my fuck faces are more intense. She's sucking and licking my clit so fuck'n good, I can't help but to explode all my sweet honey in her mouth. I look at you and we all crawl to you. Your dick is standing at attention and you have this look of a tiger in your eyes, as if we were prey and you are ready to devour us.

You lay on your back as I climb on top of you and start riding your roc hard dick while one girl is riding your face, and the other two are eating each other's pussies. I get off you and we all start sucking your dick and balls. You start fucking one of the girls in her ass in the mix of watching me lick the pussies of the other girls. The moans are driving you crazy... finally, you buss your nut all over her ass." (4/5/22, 7:38PM)

Terria: "My love, babe oh goodness, I was fiend'n for yo ass tonight. I love it when we are getting along and loving each other. I love it when you're happy. It makes my heart melt when I hear you laugh. I can even feel when you're smiling ear to ear without seeing your handsome face.

I had to bring out the purple monster and I drifted into a light sleep for a few minutes with the purple monster still in my hand. Lol! I had to get up and wipe myself up. I got back into the bed and now I'm sitting up to write you this letter with a few pics attached. I love you so much Adore, and that will never change no matter what we go through. I love you till death do us apart. I honestly can't see myself living life without you.

I mean can't you tell??? I was crying so damn hard the other day. I couldn't barely see while driving. I really thought I was about to lose you. I didn't know what I would do without you. I need you. I'm going to always need you. I can see if we don't speak for a day or two, but that's it! Bring your ass here and give your wife sweet kisses with them sexy juicy ass lips of yours. Those lips bet not kiss another woman besides the women in our family. I'll fuck you up, and the bitch up, if you EVER plant your lips on another woman. Anyways, I love you babe FOREVER!!!" (4/7/22)

Nika: "Good morning. I hope yesterday went by smoothly for you. And I am not that funny, Lol. But I'm serious. I don't like to be told what to do, controlled, or any of that crazy shit. I'm already a stubborn person, so just imagine if I get pissed off! I've never had it happen but I was just letting you know upfront what I don't like. As a matter of fact, my mom used to damn near beat my ass every day of my childhood for talking back. Idk what it is, but I just don't like to be told what to do.

Now being submissive in my eyes is totally different. I have yet to have a man whom I was submissive to. I'm just the type of woman who doesn't do things just because. People have to be VERY deserving of things on a more personal & serious spectrum. For example, with my ex, he was boring and he was basically just a lost soul when it comes to relationships.

Even when I told him about the things I wasn't happy about and even gave the nigga suggestions on how to make things better. He still didn't switch up his ways. Like never planned date nights, trips, or just basic relationship shit. I told him if I wanted a nigga to lay up with every now and then, then its plenty to choose from. Lol. Shit suppose to be different in relationships. He was a good dude as far as not cheating and being respectful or whatever, but he lacked everywhere else. All he did was talk about work and his family.

I use to tell him that I don't give a damn about none of that. Lol. He would still talk about it. Honestly, most women would settle because of a man not cheating, but not me. We weren't connected on a mental or spiritual level, so I fell back and let go.

I said that to say this, I felt like he wasn't catering to me mentally, emotionally, or spiritually, and he didn't put in any effort to do so. So as a real woman, my soul wouldn't allow me to be submissive to someone like that. I didn't feel 100% secure or safe with him, I didn't feel like if needed, he would be able to take lead and I'd be able to trust his lead without question.

He just wasn't it! This might be TMI, but he had the audacity to send me pictures of lingerie off a website, basically wanting me to wear it for him. I told him he wasn't deserving of that kind of treatment. Like he wasn't doing ANYTHING to make me want to do something like that for him. Lol.

Right now, I'm not even wanting a relationship. I just want to focus on advancing in my day trading career, and achieving my goals. Basically I just want to make this year all about me. More self-love, self-care, & self-growth.

In all honesty, the conversations you and I have had, has been more interesting and entertaining than any conversation I've ever had with my ex. That is so crazy because I've known him over 10 years but got into a serious relationship last year. So far, you seem like a really down to earth and cool person. And I peeped that you talk around subjects that you don't want to give direct answers too, Lol. But me being me, I'll just turn around and ask again until I get an answer! I guess its a Libra thing, Lol.

But yeah, I don't want to mislead you or anything. Have you thinking we're going to be together. As of now, I don't mind being your friend. If you're pursuing any relationships or have anything serious going on, don't hold back because of me. I can't guarantee that I won't be with someone by the time you're released. Even if I am and things are still going good with us, I wouldn't mind meeting you and still continuing a friendship. If I'm not with someone when that time comes, and we spend time with each other and if we feel like we want to pursue something more than just a platonic relationship, then I'll be for it.

And yeah I caught that, 'take control' comment! Lol. Well I love a man who knows how to take control. I must admit that I am attracted to you. So yeah yesterday when you said you were sexually attracted to me, a few visions went thru my mind, Lol. And why are they half-ass fixing the computers? I know that's annoying af. I will try to set up a video call for tomorrow. I look forward to speaking with you later."

(4/7/22)

Nika: "Hey! Although we literally just got off the phone I decided to message you anyways! Don't ever think that you bore me. I love our conversations. Hearing about your life before incarceration means a lot to me. It gives me insight of you. I know that you've been incarcerated for a long time, but it seems to me that you haven't just wasted that time. Like you've tapped into your purpose on this earth and discovered & developed your talents. I can appreciate that about you. You're mature which is a major plus. And trust me, maturity does not come with age. I know some 50-60 year olds acting like 20 year olds.

I want to thank you for lifting me up whether I need it or not. I know you're not here physically but you're definitely catering to me mentally. A mental connection is everything to me. Its something I have never really truly experienced. Then its like our talents align together & we both love our black people and want to see them thrive, which is another major plus. I can talk to you for hours and not get bored.

We have so much in common that I don't think boredom or problematic situations would ever be an issue with us. I don't want to speak too soon you know, because its only been a few days of consistent conversation. We have yet to experience each other during times of frustration, sadness, anger, and so on. We haven't even had a disagreement yet, Lol. So that's why I say I don't want to speak too soon because I don't know how those situations will play out? I can imagine it won't be the worst case scenario either way.

Only reason I say that is because of what you told me. You basically said for me to communicate with you no matter what the problem may be and you'll listen to me. That was a MAJOR turn on. Communication is everything to me. I have a way of expressing myself, and for someone to actually listen with an open mind and then be willing to compromise to mend whatever the situation may be, omg... that means the world. I hate arguing and I hate immature fights. I'm all about happiness. Whether we're friends or more, that mature level of communication needs to be there at all times. I'll do the same with you.

I love how you spoke on your mom. But did you really mess up your hair TWICE?! To the point of having to have a bald head, lol. Hilarious, and you already know black moms give no fucks about letting you sit out of school because of your appearance, lol. You taking ya ass to school regardless.

I had one incident similar. I had long pretty hair to the middle of my back. I was in the 6th grade and had washed & blow dried my hair. My mom wasn't home to clip my split ends, so I called and asked her if my cousin, (who was also in the 6th grade) could clip the ends for me. My mom said 'no.' My hard head ass let her anyways. Man when she got done, my hair was like an inch past my ears. My mom beat my ass so bad, lol. I never let anyone else cut my hair after that.

As far as having people to push you, I didn't have that support either. I was so good in basketball. The love I had for the sport was everything. Around the time I got in middle school, my parents started having marital issues. My dad is a truck driver so he almost never made it to my games, but he was big on sports and we'd watch the college and NBA games together when he was home. However, my mom knew nothing about sports so she never came to my school games or even supported the fact that I loved the sport.

Its like when you see your parents not giving a fuck, then eventually you stop giving a fuck. That's what happened with that. They ended up divorcing like a year afterwards. I just knew I would have the best years of basketball during my actual school years. I was looking forward to it. I played rec basketball, and our team won the state championship two years in a row. When I say I loved that sport, it was like a first love to me.

My cousins on my mom's side all played sports and set records that have yet to be beat in the schools, in football, track, and basketball. Unfortunately, by the time I became of age to play in the schools, they all were in college or had graduated college and moved from our hometown. So I literally had no support.

I can tell that you are very passionate about art. I'm happy that you are. It lets me know you're living in your purpose, and you have something to look forward to. Like I cannot stand a lost soul. People who don't even have a clue and don't tempt to even find a clue, lol. They're just taking up space. Like when you try to help them, they become defensive, thinking someone is judging them or talking down on them. I can't blame everyone who has that mindset, but at some point, they have to open their minds and stop making excuses for themselves.

Thank you for giving me a little background about yourself. You definitely had a lot going for yourself. I can tell you wasn't just out here bullshitting around. You actually took effort into advancing yourself and taking up a trade. I just hate the situation that transpired which led to your incarceration. I would like to know more about it, but only when the time is appropriate and you're ready to speak on it. No pressure. But your time there is nearing the end so we only can look forward and keep pushing forward. I'm sure you have a great future ahead of yourself. You're definitely a King and on top of that, an awesome person. So you will win in life and don't let anybody tell you anything different. Even if you ever feel discouraged. Just know that you got this.

Ughhh, I didn't want to speak on this but I am anyways. Lol. It is so hard to completely stray away from sexual or flirty conversations with you. Lol. I know how dudes are. A woman can tell a guy a million times that she wants a platonic relationship but as soon as she gets flirty, it's an automatic perception that she wants more and the guy starts to think its an opportunity for him! And he may possibly have the idea that they are more than just friends. I'm doing everything within my control to not mislead you, but I can be flirty at times, lol. But yeah, if it ever comes a time that anything happens, (per your previous message) please do take your time with me. I want to take in every second of the moment, feel every sensation of your touch, and enjoy the overall experience. Just to let you know, that wasn't being flirty, I'm serious.

I don't know why I'm so comfortable with speaking on that to you. Seriously, from the time I saw your picture or whatever, I had an immediate connection with you. One that I seriously tried to ignore & fight. This is so strange to me but just remember if it ever gets to that point, definitely take your time. I don't know the true purpose of coming across each other, but I do know we're meant to be in each other lives for a reason. More than likely I'll probably speak to you on the phone before you actually receive this message, since its pretty long. Either way, & as always I look forward to speaking with you again. Ttyl." (4/8/22)

Nika: "I forgot to add my business logo pic on the last message so here it is! The circle logo, I use as stickers to brand & package my items. I'm sending you a throwback pic from last year too. I was in Mexico with my best friend for her birthday." (4/8/22)

Nika: "I'm not going to flex like I'm not feeling you, because I am. But I also know from previous situations, its best to keep everything on a slower wavelength. Don't wanna move too fast. After we got off the phone around 11:30PM, I was okay at first. But a few minutes went by and I was like dang=0(. I really want to talk to him some more. I was legit missing ya ass, lol. Like seriously. Then you called again like an hour later and I was so happy. You just bring like a joy to me. Really, I can't even explain it but it makes me happy.

Now that I've gotten that out my system, shall I move on and address your latest message?! I saw where you said you want me to 'try my very best to respect' you. And I assume the all caps were emphasis. May I ask, did I say anything to you that came across as disrespectful? Did I offend you or something? The way that part of the message was worded, it seemed like you took offense to something. Or maybe its just me? But please address. Just know that I'll always give you the utmost respect. So far, from what I've seen, you deserve it. I always look forward to conversing with you.

For the record, no matter how spoiled I am or how much I'm used to having my way, I will always be fair. Besides, if I can push you around, then I don't want any dealings with you, period. But I am also enjoying the start of this, or should I say us!

Never would I ever try to change you. Hopefully you wouldn't try to change me either. However, like you said, 'change sometimes can be good, especially if its going to elevate us.' And just so you know, this message was supposed to go out around 2AM. I had gotten intoxicated and decided to stop and finish later today because I realized I was typing crazy stuff, lol. I was like hell nah, I'm tripping. Let me erase that & save to drafts bc I'm doing too much.

Yes we have something really special. I've always let go and let God. Especially when it comes to things that I know I have no control over. One of the last times that I let go and let God, is when I came across you on that website. I don't know how long I was going to just sit on your contact info. Like after I came across you the second time on that website, I was like okay, I'm fighting by trying not to reach out to him, so let me just add him on Jpay so I'll have your info saved in case I do decide to reach out one day.

Then a few days later once you actually reached out... I was like okay, this is a sign, hopefully a good one, and so far it has been. Honestly, I did not know that you could see that I added you. I don't know if you've seen that website or not but its literally like a hundred small photos on each page. For some reason I only saw your pic. Shit is sooooo dang weird. I'm very in tune with my intuition but I tried to fight it so hard. Its not because you are incarcerated, but because I'm very skeptical of meeting people online. I've only done that once which was over 10 years ago. But I only did it because the person lived like 30 mins away, which was still a risk. He is also the same dude that I recently broke up with, lol.

I don't doubt that you have a lot of positive things going on for yourself. I can tell you're a very self-proficient person and definitely looking forward to the impact you'll have once released. I'm all for your growth as well as mine. Although we both have an artistic side to us, I love how you show interest in the other things that I have going on, like the day trading & stock market. That may be something you'd like to get into one day. If so, just know at first its going to be confusing as hell looking at those charts with a bunch of green and red lines. But once I break it down to you, you'll be like really, that is so simple.

I practice on demo trading accounts a lot. Practice makes perfect. Hopefully by the end of summer, I'll be able to attain a huge number of trading capital thru this company I'm trading with. I will be able to trade bigger lots, take bigger risks, and make bigger profits. The bigger the risk, the bigger the losses & wins, whichever way the trade goes. The company I'm working with now basically puts up the capital for me to trade, and I split my profits with them. Honestly, I really do have a crazy love for the market. Its one of my passions and I see it being a major pay off in the future.

To me, luxury is time, freedom, and not having to dwell on a dead end job. It's being able to travel whenever, wherever, and spending all the time possible with the ones I love. It's having a piece of mind. Also, being able to sow back into my community, the black community. I want to build up the black neighborhoods, and especially build up the children. They need the right guidance. That's my type of luxury. But I love to spend too, so unlimited shopping is going to be a God send, lol. I'm consistently working towards that stage of my life, but also patiently awaiting my time. God's timing is better than mine. All I can do is continue to put in the work and allow God to do His part. I trust in Him.

Like I mentioned, the basis and foundation is still the same, just modernized or advanced, and of course swag has changed. Everybody is wearing tighter clothes now. Which I think looks a lot better. The only thing I don't care for is the music. Too many mumble rappers and R&B isn't exactly R&B

anymore. I was raised during the 90s, so I'm really big on Tupac & his era. He's my favorite rapper, poet, or whatever else you may consider him. He was always speaking knowledge that didn't just educate you, but actually took your mind to another level of deep thinking. But of course the south blew up and took over round the 2000s, so I'm very big on our music. Who are some of your favorite rappers or musicians? I know you're into music, so you'll probably have quite a few! I was heavily into music starting from the children's church choir.

But I have quite a few family members who are into music. My stepbrother had a whole studio in our home. I hated it, lol. Niggaz in and out the house all damn day. Music blasting 24/7, it was awful. I never got any rest. Only reason I was living there is because I had a vehicle accident, lost everything, had to go thru 2 years of physical therapy and get back on my feet. I would get out bed interrupting their recording sessions cussing them str8 out and I mean bad. Like our rooms were next door, I didn't want to hear that shit 24/7, I had to stay fully clothed at all times.

Like I couldn't even step out my room without seeing niggaz literally passed out on the floors and living room couches. Then they started eating my food out the refrigerator, so you know I went off. Lol. I'm going on too bad. These flashbacks make me wanna call my brother and cuss him out right now??? I know you probably wondering where were our parents? My daddy pretty laid back, he always on the road because he drive trucks.

My stepma real cool, she didn't give a damn. She would go in her room and shut the door and tune everybody out. She fussed at them a few times but they didn't take her serious at all. I didn't live with my mom because at the time she was living in (another state) and besides, we clashed too much. I was like 20 years plus around this time.

No need to spoon feed me first. Lol. Give it to me straight, no fiter. I can handle it ALL. Trust me. As far as my inner thoughts, yeah, you're not ready for that. I'm going to have to spoon feed you first!!! See how that can go both ways? Lol. I might give you a little insight here and there but just know that they are there, a lot of them. I won't hold back. I'll inform you when the timing is appropriate depending on which inner thoughts I want to share with you." (4/10/22)

Considering I was going through some very rough times with Terria, my emotions were all over the place. Terria's negative transferred energies made it harder for me to elevate with Nika. I had become immune to Terria's lies and disrespect. One of my first request for Nika was in regards to Nika trying her "very best to respect me." Unfortunately, Nika was unaware of the negative energy I was embracing from Terria, which is why Nika asked me, "may I ask, did I say anything to you that came across as disrespectful?"

The truth is... no, Nika hadn't "offended" me at all. My words towards Nika was a reflection of my own guilty silhouette. I had not mastered the art of concealing my true emotions, therefore, my emotions transferred over to Nika. Terria isn't a good liar, Terria is A GREAT LIAR, and I will be the first to admit, Terria's "humble words and increased preparations" blinded me... momentarily.

{"Humble words and increased preparations are signs that the enemy is about to advance"} Sun Tzu.

Terria: "Babe, I woke up thinking how I wanted to get fucked by you yesterday and you had to get off the phone. I was like, GOT DAMMIT!!! But you already know, you gave me some fire ass head babe. You were tongue kissing my clit just like I like it. Thank you my love. Lol! Of course, I sucked your dick with no hands until you came in my mouth. I LOVE YOU SO MUCH BAE AND MISSING YOU LIKE CRAZY BABE!!!

So today I'm going to dance class at 11:00AM and then Ya'sha and I are going to the spa to get waxed in those intimate areas (vajacial and vagina steam) and all that stuff. Now, a vajacial is just a facial for the vagina. After getting it waxed, she puts a vagina mask on it, then clean and scrap the dead skin from off top and make it look pretty. Lol!!!

Trust me babe, your woman have some good sweet juicy tight pussy waiting for you. Lol!!! Shit, we might throw in a massage too. But today I just want to pamper myself babe. Then I was going to eat some seafood tonight. So that's my day today. So I hope you have a wonderful day today babe and just know, I'm always thinking about you and can't wait to be with you." (4/11/22)

Nika: "Hey! It was great talking to you earlier. I just received another one of your messages. Yes, technology has allowed us to type the things that we cannot say. I've always been better at expressing myself thru writing than over the phone. It allows me to dig deeper into my thoughts and clearly process things. Sometimes I can get emotional or whatever & its hard to fully express myself over the phone.

But in person its going to be a lot different. Its not often that I do get emotional, but if I do just take it as a sign that I really care for you. Its crazy that you said it seems as if I'm right there because it literally felt like that last night after we talked, and I was thinking about you. Idk what's going on, never felt like this before or experienced anything like it.

Some of the things that you speak on as far as our possible future together, have already crossed my mind. This shit is kinda scary if I'm going to be honest. The way you think, such as how you move and like to be low key is exactly how I like to move. Even when you said as long as we have an understanding about us, then you know how to play your role. I swear I'm the same. I just need proper communication & clear understanding so I can know how to go abt my role.

You mentioned I'm like your breath of fresh air, I feel the same about you. Like I went from being in a relationship with someone who clearly didn't understand me or connect with me on a mental level at all. That was draining af. You know the physical is good and everything, but if I'm not mentally connected then what's the point? Not having that connection with a person effects everything. I lost complete interests in him and moved on like he never existed. I don't understand how ppl can actually be with someone and marry someone but still have a big ass void within their relationship. I just can't settle. I want legit happiness, not any fake shit.

Now since I've been talking to you, I connect with you so well on all levels. So I can only imagine the physical. Even though I don't know you like that, I can visualize a future with you. Your mindset, your love for art, how you said you have a real appreciation for freedom now, and just so much more. This let's me know you're going to give life your all, and do everything possible to make sure you keep your freedom once you're home. Basically it just let's me know you're living with purpose, you're not lost. You have vision and you believe in yourself. Nothing about you whatsoever says weak or follower.

I know you didn't ask for details of my past relationships or how I was with past relationships, but I'd like to share anyways! I've had 3 boyfriends. The 1st one was too overprotective and tried to be controlling once I gave him my virginity.

His ways didn't work with me. I was raised differently. He was 19, I was 15, lasted for 4 years. Second relationship happened as a joke. My Grandma just had gotten buried and I had met a dude the exact same day. He wasn't even my type. Grammar all off and he was drinking a 40 and hanging over a damn fence?? I feel so ashamed right now.

Anyways, I was vulnerable and lost af without my Grandma. So I start kickin it with him. We partied together, made plays together, and was together 24/7 damn near. His family fucked with me strong and everything, it wasn't no sex or anything. But I've always been a person who loves a challenge. His girlfriend was accusing us of being together. She came at me sooooo wrong, so I told her straight up, 'bitch I'll take ya man,' and I did. In the long run the joke was on me, so I pick my challenges wisely now, lol. He was an alcoholic and had no real ambition in life. Like he was always on hot boy shit. I ended up leaving him after 3.5 years. However, while we were living together, I had broke up with him and we were just roommates until I moved out.

I did have a friend that I was close too. He & I kicked it for like 7 years on & off. Basically when I was single, I was with him. But we had a crazy bond so we would just pull-up on each other from time to time just to talk, smoke, or go out.

Never was always sexual. He is like 8-9 years older than me. I learned a lot from him as far as the game. We were very low key. Only a handful of ppl knew about us. I never brought drama his way & he didn't bring it my way.

I had one other friend that I was also cool with. He's 9 years older than me. I was dealing with him while I was with my 2nd boyfriend (Pawn). Pawn was a cheater, straight up, lol. I told him I didn't want him anymore but he refused to let me go. So I played along only because at the time he could provide for me financially. But I told him while he be out with whoever, just know I'm out too. So I basically had 2 boyfriends. They both took care of me. Anyways, all my actual boyfriends were at least 3-4 years older.

For the record I never ran the streets or was a ho. I never ran thru family members or homeboys. Never been the drama type. Never ran with crowds. Even when I was a lost soul I still had class about myself. I did have a wild streak for a few years because I was suffering from the death of my grandmother. I didn't know how to grieve. It broke me and turned me into a stranger. Like I didn't know who I was anymore.

I was clubbing damn near every day of the week, getting high, (I've only ever smoked weed, nothing else) drinking, and just living day to day with no purpose. With my family, I love them sooooo much but I've witnessed them talk about other family members, so I know they do the same with me. I haven't asked nobody for shit in over 6 years. If I go thru struggles, I go thru it by myself, but I never give up.

I'm secure with who I am and who I once was. I have no regrets. As for this thing called 'life,' I just want to be happy.

I've had my fun even tho I was a very lost individual during my fun stage. All I want now is to build. I'm not into entertaining multiple dudes or playing with people's hearts. I'm a really good person and I do believe that God favors me.

Through all I've been thru, I'm still here and blessed. Not once did I give up on myself or feel sorry for myself. I kept moving and going because self-pity will only delay the blessing laying ahead. There have been times where I have pushed myself so hard, and for a long duration of time, to the point that I became mentally burnt out. I've learned not to do that. I have my days where I'm just so freaking overwhelmed that I lock myself in the closet, cry, let it all out, wash my face and return like everything is okay.

My cousin put me on to IG. I started an online business, it was booming like hell to the point I moved my ass out my parents house into my own house, got another car, and was doing really good for myself. Like, all those blessings was just pouring in. I'm just happy I'm at the point in life now where I'm not confused. I'm not questioning myself. I know exactly what I want and how I want it. I work hard towards my goals and the lifestyle I want to have. I'm not where I want to be, but I know exactly where I'm headed. Its a process, one that I just have to trust all while keeping God as the head.

To refer to your message, you say you're all over me and I don't even know it. I been peeped that! And those kisses you sent, trust they went to every place of pleasure imaginable. Anyways, I know this message is very long, but I had to touch base on a lot of things, especially the things that shaped me into the person I am today. I know you're worth the wait. You didn't even have to mention it. Friends, friends w/benefits, or a serious relationship? Whatever we may end up being, just promise you want change. I love who you are as a person. So if the time comes to where I do completely open up and allow you all the way in, I promise to never tap out on the love you have for me." (4/11/22)

Terria: "I got your pictures and boy oh boy, you are so got damn sexy babe! Every time I look at your pics or see you on video I say to myself, 'I can't wait to have this sexy ass man all to myself'. You make me so horny because you always have this look of desire and seductiveness and its such a FUCKN turn on bae. My goodness! You drive me nuts in a good way, lo! I don't know what's going to happen when we first touch, but I can sense how magnetic and electrifying and intense its going to be. Can you imagine?

You know sometimes I be in deep thought and I ask myself, 'am I really living? Whom am I living for? Is it for me or others?' Because I do believe we've all been here before and we live on through our ancestors. I want us to live life to the fullest babe. I want us to push each other to our full potential, when I went back to get my MBA I was scared because in the back of my mind, I was like, 'I don't think I could do it, I got way too much going on so how is this going to work?' That's what I would tell myself sometimes. But I knew I always push through because that's what I do, even through fear, through anything, I always push through.

That shit was hard but when it was time for me to walk across that stage, I was super proud of myself. I was like, 'yea, I did that,' lol, I know what I'm capable of. I don't think I've tapped into all my abilities just yet and that's where YOU come in at. You will see things in me that I can't see, and I will see things in you that you can't see in yourself. That's our opportunity to push one another to bigger and better. So with that being said, babe I love you and your happiness is super important to me. You never have to worry about me abandoning you, neglecting you, losing interest in you, etc., because no matter how bad our arguments are, we are meant to be. We are.

I LOVE YOU ADORE HSAAF, I REALLY DO BABE." (4/12/22)

READ THIS ENTIRE BOOK
READ THIS ENTIRE BOOK
READ THIS ENTIRE BOOK
READ THIS ENTIRE BOOK
READ THIS ENTIRE BOOK
READ THIS ENTIRE BOOK
READ THIS ENTIRE BOOK
READ THIS ENTIRE BOOK
GOD
LOVE
FREE
BOOK
BOOK
READ THIS ENTIRE BOOK READ
READ THIS ENTIRE BOOK READ

Nika: "Gosh, it just seems like you're a God send fr. Like its just too good to be true. I really hope what we are growing is genuine. I'm 100% sure that I'm genuine in every aspect pertaining to us. I really do have a lot of respect for you. You're different but in a good way. If only you could read my inner thoughts! Let me stop!!! Lol. Making a guy feel special such as catering to him in romantic or spontaneous ways, dressing up in lingerie, sexy lap dances (I can't really dance tho, lol) or just doing something to make him feel extra special has to be earned.

I have morals. A lot of women do this type of stuff for every nigga they end up with. I haven't did it for nobody because nobody I've been with was worth it. I had a home'girl who had just started talking to this dude. Didn't know shit about him at all. But this bitch dressed up in lingerie under a dress & went to his place. I told her she was stupid. Like he hasn't done anything, period, for her to show him that kind of appreciation. I just don't get it. They didn't last long! But forget them, you get my point hopefully?

I love to have fun and turn up but I always carry myself with class and I stand by my morals and values. Not saying I can't get ratchet because I can, and I have. I'm definitely not saying my sex isn't any good, but I will not do the extra if you're not deserving of it, or my man. Like hookups, sneaky links, or whatever you wanna call em, after its done, I'm gone.

I'm not staying around to cuddle, talk, or none of that extra shit. Not even to smoke a blunt. I'll take it home tho, lol. Like don't even call me. I'll call you if I wanna link again. I'm just like a nigga, lol. But I'm just keeping it real, don't judge me. Only my MAN (KING) will get the extra and submissiveness, if our relationship has grown to that level where I have lowered my guard, feel secure within the relationship, I will be submissive.

You asked for my turn-ons/turn-offs/likes/dislikes? I'll speak on some general things. I absolutely hate smacking. I'll throw a whole tantrum or just leave the area/place if somebody is smacking. I don't like for ppl to eat with their mouths open either or talk with food in their mouths. Certain noises I hate such as snorting then forcing mucus up the throat to spit out. I'm getting irritable thinking abt it. Hate toilet seats left up. I hate pumping gas.

If I feel like I can make it home although my gas light is on and I pass 5 gas stations on the way home, I will not stop. I'll go straight home. I hate sweeping so I actually put the vacuum on floor setting and use it. I do not like any noise whatsoever while sleeping. Music can be an exception, but eventually I'll wake up & turn it off. I like to sleep in the dark, no lights. I don't like slow or stupid drivers. I literally cuss out everybody on the road.

I do like walks in the park or peaceful quite areas, and shopping for handcraft & art supplies. I enjoy that more than shopping for clothes, but I love shopping, period. Like going to 5-10 stores and even back tracking to previous stores. I love massages, I love to take out of each day and just talk to God, or say a prayer. I'm a country girl so of course I love to ride 4-wheelers, & I enjoy horseback riding but I'm an amateur. I love the beach. I love to learn about our history & ancestors. Used to be deeply into politics, but not anymore. I like to eat, lol, I'm greedy! Mexican restaurants are my fav bc they have the best margaritas & are not shy on the alcohol. I've never been to one & left sober.

Sexually, I hate for my ears to be touched with a tongue, such a major turn off. Don't like my neck sucked so hard to the point it leaves a hickey. I like it gentle, do not like my feet in nobody mouth. -1, its disgusting -2, its not sexually stimulating -3, I'm certainly not about to do any kissing. Same position for too long is a no no! If I become less responsive, then its time to switch it up. Do not ask me to call you 'daddy' at any given time, definitely a turn off & sickening. I can't get into the details like I want to abt my turn-ons!

But I'm a talker & tend to be very noisy (moaning wise) & I like to be talked to. Not too much talking, but just enough. I like to be guided & controlled, just lead me & tell me what to do. Fav position... just depends on how blessed you are down there! I'm trying to keep this as clean as possible but its soooooo hard. Maybe we can finish the conversation over the phone without being too explicit!

You know I laughed at the way you started the paragraph after you said you loved me. Its like you was reading my mind. We're just too perfect for each other. I'm convinced at this point. But I really do appreciate you, and of course I'm still sorting through my thoughts, feelings, and everything else. So when I feel the time is right, I will speak on it more. I've been thru some fucked up situations with this love thing. So I'm very stubborn when it comes to my guards. But I really do think you can read minds. Lol. Like, I've never experienced this with anyone, period. Yes its very SCARY. You're always on point. Maybe we're connected deeper than what we realize and its gradually coming into realization.

Just to speak on myself in general, I had mommy issues. I felt unloved, resented, & despised. I grew up thinking my mom didn't love me. She actually jumped on me when I was like 12 or 13, for no complete reason. She told me to do something, and I responded 'okay,' in a normal voice, no back talk or anything. I'm so happy my dad was home that day bc he had to pull her off me. My brother was so shaken. Like, he used to laugh and pick when I got in trouble, but not that time. He was even yelling 'mom get off Nika!' I didn't even fight her back. I just tried to guard my face and body with my hands and arms. Like, she knocked me over a stereo set and everything. I didn't talk to her for like a month.

Just so happen right after it happened my older cousin pulled up in our yard. I told him what happened and he took me to our Grandma house. You better believe my grandparents showed their ass on her bc they didn't play about me at all. They wouldn't even let me go back home for days or let her come see me. My Granddaddy told her if she ever put her hands on me again like that, that he would put his hands on her. He was pissed. I had never seen him like that.

My mom drank alcohol a lot and heavily. She was a functioning alcoholic because she always kept a job. But I would find beer bottles and cans hid in her bathroom. She drank malt liquor a lot. To this day she still drinks but not like she did back then, it was awful. I've never had that mother/daughter relationship with her. That's why its so easy for me to go months without even speaking to her. Like, I don't be feeling no type of way about it either. She has apologized for how she treated me growing up, and asked me to forgive her. I did forgive but its so hard to forget.

The black community doesn't believe in speaking up or going to a therapist. We'd rather keep all of our hurts and traumas bottled up which only messes up generation after generation. That cycle has to stop. We have to learn to deal with our hurt so we can heal from it. I know most men judge women & treat women accordingly to their moms. So its understandable that you felt you could never trust a woman from an early age. Hopefully that perception changes.

I just want you to know that if we do become one, you'll never have to question my love or loyalty. I would never put you in a position to even think to question it. If I'm not happy about something then I'll communicate that with you & vice versa. If we can mend the situation ourselves then good, if not, then we can go to therapy together.

At the end of the day I just want something real, and I want happiness. Like no cheating or sneaky shit. Idc what issues may occur from attitude, schedules, to sex life, and everything in between. Just communicate it with me. I've never had a 3sum, but if that's something that we want to try one day, to spice up our sex lives, then I'm down for it. But only within a marriage! So don't get too excited. Lol. But I'm proud of you, I'm happy that we found each other. I just imagine a long successful life with you and people wondering how did we even meet. Lol." (4/13/22)

Terria: "I had a little treat for you. I brought a dozen of chocolate covered strawberries last night, along with some cool whip in the fridge. I had on the shorts you like and was ready to tease you with some lip service. Damn! Babe I was super upset. I love you Adore babe. I'm willing to do things to keep that spark going between us. We're in this forever babe." (4/14/22)

Nika: "First and foremost just know what I'm about to share goes for committed relationships only. Not hookups! However, my sex drive can be very crazy. I'm talking about literally sexing all night. Take brakes in between to smoke or whatever. But I'm not about to fuck just anyone. I do have toys. I used to sell toys thru a company called (company's name). Of course I enjoy masturbating, but I love it even more when my man (whenever I get one, Lol) watches me do it. I like to look deep into the eyes of my partner while sexing, but I always end up closing my eyes, especially if its really good. I love to utilize everything possible, the bed, countertops, balcony, bathtub, chair, even the floor. Or just turn me towards the wall, bend me over, then go deep inside my pussy. I love making my pussy grip the dick, especially as it slides in and out of me.

While getting fucked from the back, I need my ass gripped and smacked. I've never done anal, but sometimes I do like a finger (1 finger) halfway in my ass while getting fucked from behind. Kisses/licking on my neck and back during sex turns me on, but my breasts/nipples being sucked, licked, and held onto before & during penetration makes my pussy super wet.

Getting wet just thinking about it now! I have average sized (36 c) BEAUTIFUL breasts. Not too big, not too small, and perfect sized nipples. Thighs & ass thick. But I do need to work out more so I can get this ass back sitting right. Lol. Don't laugh at me! I cum a lot, like bk to bk if you know what you're doing! As mentioned in the last message, I'm noisy and love to talk nasty during sex. If we're close up missionary, I need you to talk nasty to me in my ear. Also rub my clit while fucking me in whatever position is most comfortable for you.

Something I absolutely love to do with the right person, is give head. I'm pretty good at that shit, I must admit. I like to deep-throat then swallow on the dick while its at the back of my throat so my throat can caress and massage it with each swallow. Also, I enjoy being fucked in the mouth, but not too rough. If we get to that point, I need you to make sure that you GENTLY slap & rub me in the face with your dick. I'm into freaky sex.

As long as I'm comfortable and you're comfortable, I'm down to try whatever. If its something I'm not into, I won't hesitate to let you know. At the end of the day if I'm in a committed relationship, I want to be able to please my man in every possible way. A lot of ppl don't like to kiss or whatever after oral sex. I do. I know I taste good so I have no issue with it. Like fuck my pussy good then take your dick out and stick it in my mouth.

Suck & rub my nipples while playing with my pussy, then put your fingers in my mouth. But I need you to match my energy. Like fuck me, eat me, then fuck me some more. I can make you nut by giving you head. Might take a min, but it will happen. Not a fan of nut in my mouth, but if I'm feeling it in the moment, then I'll allow it. But nutting on my face, ass, and rest of my body is always an option.

Just not in me without permission that is! For the record I don't pull hair, lol. Might grab or tug at it a little while getting my pussy ate, or during missionary sex. Another thing, I have a fat pussy so I like when my lips are spread apart and my clit is being sucked & licked. I also enjoy being tongue fucked. Just know that when I ride your dick, starting out its for your pleasure, but ends up being for my pleasure. So I can get a little wild on top.

Roleplay & sexual stimulation is a must. Like tease my body, heighten my hormones, have my body uncontrollably yearning for you. Smoking is an aphrodisiac, for me anyways, so I do like to do so b4 & during sex every now & then. Drunk or intoxicated sex, period, is unmatched, love it. But there are times where I would like for you to just bend me over, shove your dick in my pussy, and fuck me hard. Like take complete control of me & have your way with me. I like it slow & fast but its just something about slow sex because climaxing off of slow sex, you get to feel every sensation of eruption.

You asked if I wanted to be your first when you touch down. That's on you. Whatever you say goes, only for that situation tho. So don't get all big headed & feeling yourself!!! In the future if that's something you want to do then I'll come into your town, book a hotel suite, & plan accordingly. Don't make any sudden decisions right now because neither of us know where we'll stand when the time comes. Anyways, I guess I gave you a hell of an idea of what I like sexually. Didn't mention everything, but I'm sure you get the point. I would like for you to share your likes/dislikes, turn-ons/turn-offs, sexual & non-sexual. Do you have any fantasies?

I could go on and on but I'll stop there and just wait to receive your next message so I can add on to this one! Okay, so I just received your message. It's safe to say that I really don't have to add on to this one. Seems like we're on the same page AGAIN." (4/14/22)

Terria: "You want me to type 3 things that I would like you to try and work on within our relationship/future marriage?

#1. I want you to STOP talking at me. For example, if I don't do something you asked me to do, you talk to me like a child just to reprimand me which makes me feel like a joke or weak, so I get defensive and be ready to go off. I know I'm used to having my way and you don't like that but damn! You don't have to handle me like that babe. Because just like I mentioned earlier, I'm sensitive and feelings get hurt because its coming from you, and I hate disappointing you. I like how you talked and explained in regards to me stopping the money from coming through. You didn't talk at me, you talked to me, it clicked and I immediately felt horrible about that. I would never in my life do that again.

That conversation made me feel like you were sitting next to me holding my hand, giving me eye contact, talking to me and letting me know how my actions affected you. We hugged it out at the end. That's how I felt. I wish every conversation made me feel that way but I know that's not going to happen.

#2. Don't be so quick to shut me up when I'm talking, just because I might be saying something you don't agree with. It makes me feel like what I have to say is invalid, and I'm only good for doing exactly what you want me to do. If I have a different opinion then its irrelevant. Can you please try hearing me out?

#3. Can you work on not expecting so much out of me in a short period of time? Then you always say, 'bae, I know you have a lot on your plate and I appreciate you,' but then you say 'I need you to get focused because this isn't a game'. As if I'm the one playing them. I do take what you need done seriously babe. Sometimes I really get overwhelmed and check out. You go 100 miles an hour on the phone saying you need me to get 'this,' 'that,' and 'this done,' and I'll be like uumm okay.

My anxiety kicks in and I shut down. I need you to really be realistic on what it is you need me to do, and we can have a goal date on when I need to have it done by. Don't just pile everything on me at once and expect results, because its just me babe. I'm only one person babe, so please keep that in mind. Now let me respond to your answers and what you asked me to work on. Here's what you said.

#1. Your anger... when you get upset with me, can you please TRY not to get too upset so fast?

My Response:

That's true and I really do need to work on that babe. I really do need to be more mindful and think before I speak. I agree babe.

#2. Your submissiveness, (oh my goodness, I can hear you talking shit now, Lol) but seriously though, sometimes I need to hear that 'yes Daddy' or 'whatever you desire KING'. Basically, just work on making me feel a little more appreciated from your end. Trust, I know you do love me sincerely, but its cool to make me feel like I have the lead sometimes. Again, be a little more submissive for me... but mean it when you do it, don't just do it just because. Acknowledge me as your KING, your true KING, thank you Queen, I love you.

My Response:

To be submissive is really asking a lot from me. I don't even like that word because it can easily get abused. To be submissive is something that is earned and not given. Just like respect. I will not be submissive to you until you're out of prison, and able to fully earn it. But what I will do is respect you in a way 'YOU' want to be respected. When you're sweet to me, I can 'Yes DADDY' and when I greet you on the phone, I can say peace King or I love you King. I can do that without hesitation because you are my KING as I am your QUEEN.

#3. It would be nice if you would try to keep me involved with more of Our businesses, etc. You started off telling me about certain things concerning our businesses, credit cards, etc., and yes I know you make your own money, pay your own bills, etc., but just keep me up to date. Make me feel important as well, allow me to add on to what we already have going on, don't sleep on me Queen. I know I have a strong Queen by my side, and I know you know how to get to dem bags, and I salute you for being a hard Grinder, Networker, etc., but I also need you to understand that you are not alone. You not only have a life partner with me, but also a Business Life Partner.

My Response:

Ok babe, my bad. I do understand where you're coming from my love. I will shoot you an email once a month, showing and explaining what's going on with our accounts and what's what. I will even send yo ass the bills that are being paid from our accounts, lol. So keep up, lol. I will send you this information on the 1st of each month my love. Will that be ok?

Also, let me touch on a few things:

I know we said we're in this for life but even then, there's boundaries we should not cross or there will be consequences... some reversible and some irreversible. I love you babe, but if I'm not cool with something, I'm not doing it. PERIODT! What we will do, (IF YOU NEED IT THAT BAD) we'll figure out an alternative and discuss. For example, if you want to go in my virgin asshole, we try it and its just not doing it for me, but you really want to fuck in the ass, then we'll get you a bitch you can fuck in the ass. Lol! But you not fucking bitches just because you feel like it, PERIODT! Because the consequences to being that foolish is irreversible. There's no coming back from that.

Also, I KNOW I HAVE THE BEST GIFT OF ALL BABE... YOU!!! To be honest bae, after reading your letter, I understand you a lot more and how and why you feel the way you do. I now see how your mood goes from hot to cold when you get to talk to me. I now understand how important my presence is to you, whether its via phone or through email.

WOW! I'm so sorry babe! Listen babe, you are my priority, and as much as I would love to stop the hands on the clock just to spend time with you, sometimes life out here gets in the way. But I need you to know, I will NEVER toss you to the side my love, I need you bae. You are like no other man I've met in my life. I believe in you and what you stand for. I'm going to always rock for you and with you. Don't ever think you are meaningless to me because you're behind them walls.

You inspire me everyday to push a little bit more. You did that! Babe, I'm sorry for making you feel like you're doing everything wrong. That's not the case. I think I know what it is? We are from different worlds and we're just trying to break each other in to get familiar with each other's ways of living.

So we're going to have to really work hard and be more understanding and patient with each other, in order for this to work. I can honestly say, I'm all in babe. Babe I hope this gives you a little clarity of my intentions with our relationship. I LOVE YOU BABE AND DON'T FORGET YOU MEAN THE WORLD TO ME." (4/15/22)

Nika: "Hey Adore! Just want you to know that I missed you today. I'm getting very used to our routine. But I understand the circumstances of our situation, and I know there will be days and possibly weeks that I won't be able to talk to you. But I am happy that I got to speak with you on the video visitation this morning.

This is just sooooo freakin weird to me, but like a good weird. I just can't grasp the fact of how I feel for you... & all so sudden. Just please don't take advantage of me because you know I'm really feeling you. Like, my first attraction to you wasn't on any sexual type stuff. I WAS ATTRACTED TO YOUR MINDSET, DEMEANOR, INTELLIGENCE, PASSION FOR YOUR TALENTS, and how you RESPECT ME and take time to really get to know me.

However, I am sexually attracted to you though! Like you're putting me first & making me a priority despite the circumstances. So I can only imagine the lengths you'd go once you're home.

I just really hope it isn't a season situation, but a lifetime situation instead. That's why everything is soooo scary to me. Like I don't want to grow this great solid bond with you just for us to part ways, whether its on good or bad terms. The only thing I can do is trust God with one! I'm not doubting you, but its a whole different world out here now.

Once you're home & get a taste of the world as it is today, you're entire perspective of US will probably be different. Maybe you'll have a change of heart about everything we've ever discussed or agreed on.

I'm at the point of my life where I'm career focused, and past the phase of playing games. Next relationship I get in, I want it to be my last. My end goal is to be with someone that's loyal and I can trust, grow old with, enjoy life with, & travel the world with. I want a big ass house, well... mansion. I want to own multiple properties, businesses, & nonprofits that serves our communities. I dream BIG so I work hard. I'm not settling for no average ass lifestyle. Whoever I end up with, their vision needs to match mine or be even bigger than mine." (4/15/22)

READ THIS ENTIRE BOOK
READ THIS ENTIRE BOOK
READ THIS ENTIRE BOOK
READ THIS ENTIRE BOOK
READ THIS ENTIRE BOOK
READ THIS ENTIRE BOOK
READ THIS ENTIRE BOOK
READ THIS ENTIRE BOOK
READ THIS
READ THIS ENTIRE BOOK
READ THIS ENTIRE
GOD
LOVE
FREE
READ THIS ENTIRE BOOK
READ THIS ENTIRE BOOK READ
READ THIS ENTIRE BOOK READ
THIS ENTIRE BOOK READ

At this point, all I could do is sit back and compare Terria to Nika, or vice versa. Either way, I was starting to feel the pressure. As Terria began to infest reasons of clarity, so did Nika. Both women had their own unique individual characteristics, as well as their fair share of negative sides. Trust, I know no one is "perfect," and I wasn't searching for a "perfect woman." Soooo... why did it seem as if these women were both looking for the "perfect man"? Did they both forget that they reached out to me through an online site that informed them that I was currently incarcerated? Regardless, at this point I had the complete option to pick and choose which direction to go... " left," or "right"?

Nika: " Hello. I hope you've had a good day so far. Thanks for the encouraging messages. Honestly I cut off all negative people a long time ago. I only communicate with 3 of my friends, 2 of them I might talk to once or twice a month. If people aren't on my level or have a bigger than life vision, I keep my distance from them. My best friend since kindergarten, we talk every day, we add value to each other's lives. I quit pouring into people a long time ago, family included.

Everyone always asking me for this and that, but don't even check up on me. They just always have their hands out, I've literally given them my last. Just last year I cut my aunt off because I was taking care of her since 2016, she's ungrateful and an alcoholic. Last year I decided to put myself first and work on my goals, and of course life has been better.

I've been through a lot and go thru struggles every now and then, but I don't make any excuses for myself, play victim, or none of that bullshit. I keep pushing forward. I'm my own cheerleader & encourager, but now that I have you

I'm grateful. Trust me, I know you're worth everything, if I felt differently we wouldn't have lasted this long.

I fully understand that I love you. But I have all these mixed feelings and emotions going on that when I hear it, it makes me feel a certain way. Mentally I'm just not able to handle the phrase itself right now. I just have some healing to do. I don't want to call the phrase 'I love you,' trauma, but I would be lying if I said I didn't experience traumatic situations behind those 3 words.

As far as the messiness & drama, never been that type. I might pop my shit a lil bit if necessary, but never too many words, just action if necessary. I don't surround myself with those who would jeopardize my peace or have me in crazy situations. I'm very particular with who I'm around. I'm quiet & observant around people I don't fuck with like that, or don't know. So you don't have to worry about that kind of bullshit with me, and hopefully I won't have to worry about it with you either. Just for the record Adore, you didn't throw too much on me too soon. Everything you told me was on point, and aligns with the steps I've been taking in my life within the last year.

The only thing another man can offer me is sex. But just like I told dude that I broke up with recently, 'I'm a real woman, I need more than just dick, dick is everywhere, I can sexually satisfy myself, you need to bring more than that to the table'. He couldn't deliver, so I left. Honestly looking back, I didn't gain ANYTHING from him of value.

I'm not trying to gas you up or nothing Adore, but nobody I've ever dealt with COMPARES TO YOU. That doesn't mean you got my head fucked up or anything, I'm just being real with you. I feel like I can. Anyways, I'm about to jump back in the market and trade. I shut my door, about to put in this work. If my throat and allergies weren't messed up, I would definitely be blowing one, Lol.

I added a collage of some of my fav pics. The top one was me waiting on you to show up for the first video visitation! I had to put a sticker over my chest area on the pic beside it bc my cleavage was showing. Didn't want them to block the pic from being sent. Hope these pics hold you over until I take more this weekend. Thank you again for just being you and making life sweeter for me." (4/22/22)

Terria: "Just got off the phone with you and you talking about my energy has changed, I guess so if I've had 2 glasses of moscato and just laid back chilling. Like geesh! You always think its something bigger which be leaving me confused as hell. I'm not even looking forward to our call tonight because I just don't want to argue with you. Because all you do is tell me either how I'm feeling or if I'm supposed to be hiding something. I'on know, it just feels like I have to agree with whatever it is you're thinking just to move on from this situation.

Is that what you want? I'm sure it is, so here you go Adore. Yes, I agree with everything you said on the phone about me hiding something and lying about something. Now what that is, I have no clue so I'll sit back and let you tell me???" (4/23/22)

Nika: "Quick message! I'm going to take pics for you this week hopefully. Enjoy these in the meantime. I included a pic of me and my bestie also. So when I say (her name) you'll know who I'm talking about." (4/25/22)

Nika: "Our session is coming! But I gotta wait til my voice is back normal. I can't be moaning and sounding like some kind of animal, lol, & yes I be getting wet while talking to you. Just hearing your voice period turns me on. And when you mentioned me riding your tongue tonight... all kinds of sexual tingles & throbs went thru my pussy & nipples. I had to close my thighs tightly together to compose myself. Lol.

When the day comes, I want it to be super special. Like I don't want it to be rushed & right to it. I promise to put away my phone and focus only on us. I want us to really take our time. Foreplay, massages, rose petals, nice dinner entree, wine (I'm a big wine person by the way), good smoke, soft music, dimmed lights, jacuzzi, lingerie, and anything else you wanna add. I want it to be perfect and no holding back whatsoever. Although its easier said than done, I'll admit that I probably will hold back at first but I will loosen up as the minutes go by. If I'm fully comfortable with you, then my body will automatically and fully sexually submit to you.

I can just imagine standing & kissing, & I feel your dick getting hard. So I take my hand and gently start rubbing your dick while still kissing you. Then you start grabbing and rubbing my ass. At this point I'm working both of my hands to pull down your pants. Giving you one final kiss on your lips, I make my way down to your rock hard dick. I kiss around the head of your dick first then I start licking all around the shaft of your dick, now I'm licking and sucking your balls.

I'm getting your entire manhood wet & heightened to the fullest before I go all in and let it enter into my mouth. Now I'm still sucking your balls while slowly jacking your dick. I can hear soft moans of pleasure escape your mouth, so now I know its time to turn it up a notch. So I fill my mouth with your dick and slowly go back and forth on it. Swirling my tongue around the head every time I come back. Every time I go down on your dick I push it a little further down my throat, making my mouth wetter and wetter.

I see that you're really enjoying it so I pick up the pace just a little. Every few seconds I come off your dick to jack it, lick it, and back to sucking it. At this point its sloppy wet. So I place it between my titties and allow you to titty fuck me. I keep my tongue out so every time your dick comes up it feels the wetness of my tongue. You're wanting my pussy but I won't give it to you. I'm enjoying sucking you and licking you too much. I lie on my back on the bed and hang my head off just a little.

You walk over and start fucking me in the mouth while grabbing onto my titties. I'm playing in my pussy and you have full access to the action. I can tell I'm turning you on even more because your strokes in my mouth are getting faster. You pull out my mouth and start to rub & slap your sloppy wet dick all over my face and lips. This shit is really turning me on and my pussy is dripping wet. You're really wanting my soaking wet pussy, now, but I still won't let you enter because I want to please you only by mouth for this session.

So you slip your fingers into my wet pussy, then you put them into your mouth tasting my juices. Then you bend down to kiss me deeply. Now I'm getting up and going back to my knees to please you more with my mouth. You're jacking your dick while I'm profusely licking and sucking your balls. You're so enjoying this shit that you can't even stand straight anymore, so you back against the wall. Your dick enters my mouth again. I'm sucking faster and harder because I can feel your dick start to throb so I know what time it is. I want you to cum hard in my mouth, all over my face, and on my titties. I'm pushing your dick further and further down my throat. Your balls are being massaged with my hand, the wetness of my mouth is dripping sloppily all over your dick, thighs, and my face.

I'm going all in, I hear you began to grunt so I speed up a little more until you EXPLODE in my mouth and all over me. I'm still sucking but more gentle now until you can't take it anymore. You reach down and motion for me to get up. You start to passionately kiss me. I can feel warm chills going all thru my body, letting me know this is real love and I never want to lose you. I've fully submitted to you in ways that can't even be explained. I'm all yours. (4/28/22)

Terria: "Peace King, the reason why your letter was so much of a trigger for me was because when I was 6 months pregnant with child, my ex had the audacity to tell me he wasn't in love with me. I asked him why not? He said because I wasn't attractive pregnant. At that time, I hadn't started going back to school and getting my shit together. I was totally confused of what I wanted out of life? I was just so used to making him happy... even if that meant pretending that I didn't find other women's hair, panties, and earrings in our car. I was miserable.

This is something that I'm dealing with internally, because when I feel like someone is trying to play me, use me, or abuse me in any way, I automatically get defensive. I feel like I have to protect myself. I shut down in order to calm myself down. I can see how my shutting down can make you feel like I'm being dismissive, but its really how I cope with things that I feel will set me off.

I was able to master that when I was with my ex. Hearing your voice and reading your happy letters, somehow, makes me want to knock down this wall I've built up. That's why I was so emotional on the phone with you tonight.

Adore, I need you to know, my relationship was bad. I kept everything my ex did to me away from everyone, even my family members. All to protect him. All so he could continue to get seen in a good light. I can see how some of my actions may make you feel confused about my intentions with you in this relationship. This is why, sometimes I be feeling like we're untouchable, like our love is so strong, it makes me so anxious, nervous, happy, loved, confused, lost, smile, cry, etc.

I think I'm feeling all those emotions all at once because I'm ready for you to be home. My mind, body and soul yearns to actually be with you in the physical. It creates all these crazy emotions and I'm stuck with the question of, DAMN! What do I do with this? With something I know I can't have right now, and when I'm feeling like that, my mood changes because I'm really trying to make sense of what I'm feeling. Lol! Sometimes I be wanting you to dedicate a phone call to me, just to vent and let things that's been bothering me, out." (4/28/22)

Terria: "My Love, that letter I received from you today was not good it was AMAZING! I pictured it all and it had me moaning, super wet, and hella creative. Here's how.

I took two pillows and laid one of them flat on the bed. I took the other pillow and set it up against the head board.

Sounds crazy, but hear me out. Lol! I took the string from my sweat jacket and tired the clit sucker around the pillow. I laid flat on the bed. I took my phone and set it up on the side so I can read your letter while I do what I do. Lol! I took my pantyhose off and set on top of the clit sucker. I slightly pressed my titties against the pillow while I held on to the headboard. My pussy was super wet bae, I continued to sit on top of my clit sucker, sliding my wet pussy over the little suction cup that sucks my clit.

I bounced my ass on it as your letter got more intense after you stopped teasing me. You pinned my legs back and fucked me with your phat dickhead going deeper into my tight wet pussy hole. I couldn't help but to call out my King's name. 'Adore, babe don't stop, I love you King!' At this point, my eyes are closed, my hands are on the headboard, and my head is tilted back because I'm getting near to cum'n hard. I'm grinding harder on top of the clit sucker, my clit gets bigger, the suction cup sucks my clit in it and BOOM! I let out a super loud scream. My legs were shaking and I was out of breath. Why? I don't know so don't ask. Lol!

I set there and all I could think about is putting my wet mouth on your dick, licking around your dick head, and giving it little licks and kisses. Your dick is dripping wet and super hard. Its ready for me to take it all in my mouth with no hands. That dick taste good, and the more I suck on it the more it stretches. I slide my tongue up and down the shaft on your big hard dick. I couldn't neglect your balls, so I take my tongue that's covered with all of your dick juices, lift your balls, and suck them in my mouth.

'You like that babe, you want more babe? Don't move, let me take care of you like a King is supposed to be taken care of'. I placed my tongue directly on your perineum, and your legs immediately start to shake. I spit on your dick and put it back in my mouth.

I start sucking it so good and so hard to the point your eyes close shut and your mouth opens. Your facial expressions are getting more and more intense. 'Give me your all King, are you ready to give it to me babe?' I softly asked you. 'Fuck'n riiiiiiiight'. You replied. BOOM! There it goes, all in my mouth, dripping from my mouth and onto your dick. I lick my lips and swallow what's left. We passionately kiss and taste each other's love. Now, let's go shower and brush our teeth my love, watch a comedy and fall asleep in each other's arms." (4/29/22)

Nika: "I'm just lying in bed thinking about us. Can't wait til you're home so you can be next to me. Laid up staring in the dark smoking a fat blunt & talking about random shit. I'm asking you a million questions that you probably don't know the answer to, but somehow still end up with an answer. Lol. I can be very worrisome sometimes. We just have to be patient and remain positive about everything. Excuse me if this message is all over the place. My mind is all over the place right now! Just thinking about the future. I really look forward to sharing it with you. I hope everything goes in our favor.

Just looking back on the past month, its mainly been you who has been helping me get through my issues. You're always asking me if I'm okay and how I'm feeling. You're constantly being attentive to my feelings, emotions, and mental. Something that I'm definitely not used to but I appreciate it very much, so much so that I don't even think to ask how are you doing sometimes? I apologize. Just know that I do care about how you're doing & would like to know if anything heavy is on your mind. If its anything I can do to make your days better, please let me know.

If we do end up together and married, I promise to be the best woman and wife possible. I wouldn't expect anything less from you. I'll definitely treat you like the King you are. I feel like I already have something solid with you. Like I said, this message is everywhere! Bear with me, Lol. Just to let you know if we end up together, I'm sure people will have something to say about our age difference. But that's not going to bother me, hopefully it doesn't bother you either!!! Which I doubt it would.

I know there will be talks & whispers about us for many-many reasons. But while they are talking, we just gone continue to run up a bag & live the life they all want to but can't. We're going to be rich & happy, period. I might give you one baby and adopt about 2 more. We gon need some offsprings to run our empire once we're old & disabled, or whenever God calls us home. I want to leave behind a legacy and massive empire, just like the size of my visions." (4/30/22

Nika: "Quickie (as you say). Just want you to know that although I am working, I am very-very horny for you right now. I wish I could just sexually take advantage of you right now and have my way with you. I need to be on top of you riding your dick til I cum, as hard as possible. My pussy is so wet right now & pulsating, literally. Its just one of those days. So believe that my toys will be getting a lot of play late tonight, but I'll be thinking of you and only you." (5/4/22)

Terria: "I will continue to work towards being the best version of myself each and everyday. I want to exceed your expectations of how a Wife and Queen should take care of their Husband and King. I want nothing but the best for you, and the only way we can achieve that is to communicate effectively, in which we have been these past days. I love you Adore, I really do babe.

That good morning sex before I started my day was exactly what I needed to relax my nerves. I got in the shower first, and you followed. You're standing behind me and your dick is standing at attention. I put my face under the shower and you pull my hair back, with my head tilted back towards you... and we passionately kiss. I turn around and get on my knees, you push my head down to suck on your roc hard phat dick.

The water is splashing all over your chest, onto my face and head. You told me to 'get up' and I turn my ass to you and I put one leg up on top of the water head. I placed both hands on the glass of the shower door, and you start to fuck me from the back, deep-deep-and deeper, long dick strokes. It feels soooo good, my legs are getting weak because I can't hold it any longer. 'I'm about to cum bae,' I whispered softly in your ear. I couldn't hold back any longer, my cum decorated your dick. You felt how strong my pussy gripped your thick long dick, you tried your best to hold on a little longer----but my tight wet pussy wouldn't allow you to hold on any longer.

You fought a good fight, and the end result was your love all over me, my face, mouth, neck and lips, yummy. Now, bring me my dick babe, I want more. Sit it right on my wet tongue babe. I'm going to ride your face and let your soft wet lips spread my pussy lips apart. Taste how sweet I am babe." (5/5/22)

Terria: "My Love, I can always feel your love through your letters. You are truly one of a kind, Adore I mean that. When we talked today about my sexual encounter, I must admit, I was a little embarrassed at first. I remember that night, as if it was yesterday. This was a year after we graduated from high school, one of my best friends (GG, you'll definitely meet her) and I, were leaving to go travel a few states. We traveled to Atlanta, Texas, Chicago, LA., Nashville, etc., before another college semester started.

Well, when GG and I were in Atlanta, Crystal and a few of her friends were in Atlanta, we had no idea. GG and I were coming out of this braid shop, I had my hair braided, I see Crystal and her people walking up. We all stopped and started talking, they invited us back to her aunt's big ass home. GG and I went back home to clean up and get ready. We didn't know her aunt had a pool. GG and I were overly dressed. Lol! So they all were in the pool, so I took off my clothes and left on my thong and bra. I couldn't swim, so I got in the hot jacuzzi attached to the pool, and Crystal did too. That was my first time drinking Hennessey and coke. We started talking about old times in middle and high school, she told me she had a crush on me since middle school, and then she kissed me.

I pushed her off, I was scared that the other girls saw what we had just done. When I went into the house GG came in behind me, and was like, 'what the fuck was that Terria?' I was like, 'she kissed me'. They had like finger foods, and so everybody else came in and we all ate and laughed together.

We started kissing, and when I took a peek across the room, the other girls and GG were doing their thing. One of the other girls came over, that same girl and Crystal started taking turns licking my pussy, then they started licking it together. I sucked titties and rubbed their pussies, but I don't know, I just couldn't push myself to lick their pussies. So there you have it bae, that was the first and last time I've ever been with a woman/women. Lo! I'm sure you'll have something to say about this. Lol! Look how you got me opening up bae." (5/6/22)

Nika: "Don't even know how to start this off. Lol, but this morning was everything. I'm just waking up but feeling very rejuvenated. I was sooooo damn wet. If only you could hear how my pussy was talking back to you. I'm not going to lie, at first I was just going to do it to please you and get it out the way so I could go back to sleep, lol.

But you had me so fucking turned on that I couldn't resist getting deeper into it. Especially when you would say, 'take that dick'. My pussy was getting wetter & wetter. The entire experience made me fall for you even more. I know we both have flaws, I know every day isn't going to be the best, and I know there will be challenging times, but everything about us seems so perfect. Last night when you called I was so happy & smiling. Lol. I really did miss you. I was waiting all day just to hear your voice.

Also, thank you for understanding that I have to sacrifice part of our time just so I can work. Like I don't even have to explain it to you, because you already know, and you usually speak on it before I do. That's how I know our hustling skills together is going to be insane!

Even with just day trading and making my projects, you understand that I still need rest. Most people I know (family

& exexs) say dumb shit like 'you ain't doing nothing but sitting down putting stuff together with your hands,' or, 'you ain't doing nothing but looking at your laptop/phone all day.' They think if your job/career/passion isn't very physical that a person doesn't get tired or need rest. The human brain is the most powerful thing in this world, if they actually used theirs, they would get it.

I've cut off all negative people & cut ties with anything or anyone who doesn't add value to my life. All the distractions are gone, my conscious is clear, so I have no excuses, I am going hard. Thank you Adore, thank you for always encouraging me, making sure I'm okay, and giving me that extra push that I can use every now and then. Its the simple stuff that really matters and counts. I know you are genuine. Hope you enjoyed the session. I know I did. You were beyond awesome, can't wait til you're home. I haven't forgotten about the other message. I will get around to it very soon. I just hope you're prepared for what your eyes will read once I send it bc I'm digging into my fantasies with the next one." (5/7/22)

Terria: "So babe, one of the conversations Chera and I were having yesterday, was how one of the girls confessed that she makes her boyfriend wear a dildo because since he's been training to be a body builder, his dick shrunk. Lol! I was like, where does his dick go if he's putting on a strap on? She said, 'there's dildos made for small dick men'. Its like, the guy actually sticks his dick through the rubber dick and strap it on like that. Daaaamn! That's crazy! I wouldn't tell nobody no shit like that. I'll bring that to the grave with me. Lol! What you think bae? Would you wear one if you had to, lol!? Well I'm about to get on out of here and I'll talk to you soon I hope." (5/9/22, 4:56PM)

Terria: "Remember babe, God created Eve, specifically from Adam's ribs, which set the moral principle for marriage. Eve was to stand by Adam's side as an equal. He would love her and protect her, as if it were his own soul he was protecting. Adam and Eve were designed to complement each other, and work together. As its stated in the BIBLE, for it was 'not good' for man to be alone, together they were strong. The LORD blessed their union saying, 'therefore, a man shall leave his father and mother and be joined to his wife, and shall become one flesh'.

So, my love, this is NOT a game to me. I love you babe, don't you see that? I'm waiting for that special day to give you myself and for you to give me yourself. That day will be extraordinary babe. I belong to you as you belong to me, and that's THAT! I just want to make you happy and proud babe. Its challenging sometimes, but life is challenging and yo ass is worth any and every challenge there is to go through. You are a damn good man Adore, and I appreciate you as a man, my husband & KING." (5/10/22, 12:24PM)

Terria: "My babe be super lit... DAMN! Yo ass be on GO as soon as I say hello. Lol! I be like damn, my babe isn't gonna let me fully wake up, but that's ok babe. Your sense of humor is big and bright and I really love that about you, and how sure you are of yourself. Your beautiful ass smile that's embedded in my head, your laugh, your love for me, the way you want to provide for us, your sternness, your intelligence, your strive with getting shit done, etc., the list goes on and on and on.

I was watching 'Love After Lockup' the other day. I often wonder, if you would have enough patience to adjust to society and keep an open mind when learning and navigating within a more moderate society? I don't want you to be too overwhelmed with how much things have changed. Although, that's something that may be inevitable, then there's a possibility you will come home and immediately adapt right away. Either way, I'm not leaving your side King. I'm going to hold your hands through it all, so never try pushing me away when you're feeling a certain way.

So babe, I have some questions to ask and I've answered them already, below.

#1. What do you think the most important element is in maintaining a relationship? I think the most important thing would be TRUST. To me, a person can't have clear and open communication if there's no trust. If I don't trust you, then how will I be able to feel comfortable to open up and be myself? Trust goes a long way because if I trust you with my heart, then there's nothing I wouldn't do to keep open communication with you. The number 1 thing I look for in my Forever Partner, is TRUST. Trust sets the foundation for any relationship.

#2. What is a mistake you made in a past relationship that you don't want to repeat? It would definitely be, not to wait too long to address issues that can affect our relationship. I held on to so much pain, that same pain turned into resentment, that resentment turned into hate. I feel like if I had addressed the situation when it happened, I would have saved myself a lot of pain and disappointment. At that time of my life, I confused being a doormat for being understanding.

#3. If you could meet one celebrity, who would it be? Mary J. Blige, because I can relate to hear in many ways. Being able to rise to the occasion every single time, only pushes us more and more away from reality when there's demons you're silently fighting. That's something she went through, and to just have a moment to hug her, and sit and talk for 10 minutes would mean the world to me.

#4. If you could live inside the world of one TV show, what TV show would it be? MARTIN! DUUUUUUH! LOL! You know I love Martin bae. I can't wait to see your answers bae. Hope to hear from you soon." (5/16/22)

READ THIS ENTIRE BOOK
READ THIS ENTIRE BOOK
READ THIS ENTIRE BOOK
READ THIS ENTIRE
READ THIS ENTIRE
THIS ENTIRE
READ THIS ENTIRE BOOK
READ
GOD
LOVE
READ THIS
BOOK
READ THIS
FREE
BOOK
READ THIS
READ THIS ENTIRE BOOK
READ THIS ENTIRE BOOK
THIS ENTIRE BOOK READ
READ THIS ENTIRE BOOK READ
THIS ENTIRE BOOK READ

So much for trying to keep "equilibrium" between Terria & Nika. I was loosing my grip with Nika... and Nika wasn't even the real blame. The transferred negative energy that I allowed from Terria, quickly began to alter my relationship with Nika, in the worst ways. At first Nika was confused... soon that confusion turned into anger, anger that I had created, unbeknown by Nika. Meanwhile... Terria continued to open up doors that I couldn't ignore.

Terria: "3 birthdays ago, I flew back to New Orleans, to spend my birthday with Danyelia and a few other female friends. A guy we all went to high school with, invited us to his sex dungeon that he owns. We all were like, 'no thanks, we good,' but he gave us his business card and told us to let him know if we change our minds. He assured us that we wouldn't have to pay for admission or drinks. So we decided to go to dinner, and then this hole in the wall lounge, we all had a freaking BLAST! We were ready to go, but we weren't ready to call it a night. So Anne was like, 'let's go hit up K's spot just to go see what its about'. Oh! We were 9 deep that night. I said, 'okay, let's go sense we drinking for free.'

We got to this big grey building not too far from the French Quarters. It had this stupid huge red door with one of those huge heavy door knockers. So Danyelia did the honors, a naked white woman with heels on, opened the door. We all gave her our names, K had already paved the way, so she let us in. Shortly after we entered we walked downstairs. There, was a bar, dance floor, and strippers dancing on the pole next to a few tables, where you sit and chill at. As we looked around, we saw a few people hugging and kissing, but that was it.

We looked around but didn't see K anywhere, so we ordered some drinks and danced for a few. I saw some stairs and was like, 'let's go see what's up there'. LOL! We all nervously walked upstairs as if we already knew what to expect... no one spoke a word. For some reason my pussy was getting hella wet, I hadn't even made it to the top of the staircase. I was super nervous, anxious, and curious at the same time. As soon as we made it upstairs, all you hear is moaning and just people in the hall ways fucking and making out.

There were several see-through rooms, which gave you a front row seat to live porn in the flesh. I was stunned! I couldn't believe what I was witnessing. All of our mouths dropped to the floor. They all stood in that one spot, but I wanted to see more so I walked around. Unknown women and men felt up on me as I walked through, no, I didn't slap there hands away. I just lived in the moment.

I walked into this one room where there was this beautiful curvy woman. She was sitting up in this swing, and this man and another woman were kneeled down, taking turns licking her pussy. I walked closer to get a better view... her pussy was phat and beautiful, it reminded me of my pussy. I watched as they both ate her pussy. Her clit started to poke out of her pussy lips. I noticed the other woman grab her clit with her lips, and start to suck on it. The guy laid on his back and started licking her asshole. I couldn't resist, so I started sucking her nipples. Her moans were driving me crazy. She was begging to get fucked.

The guy finally got up and started to fuck her. His dick looked just right. It was the perfect width and length. It was made for sucking and fucking. The girl who was licking the other girl's pussy walked over and stood behind me, she proceeded to rub on my pussy. Danyelia walked in and grabbed me and yelled, 'NOT TODAY SATAN!'

Danyelia was ready to go. Lol!!! She said, 'Terria, they almost had you girl, good thing I grabbed your ass out of there'. Since that day, I've always wanted to have that exact same experience, can we bae? I'm not sure why I feel so ashamed telling you this, but I do. I just hope you don't love me any less for even thinking about going to a place like that. I LOVE YOU KING!"

(5/24/22)

Terria: "My Love, the last time we talked this much over the weekend was the very first weekend we started talking. It feels amazing babe. I'm currently feeling the butterflies in my stomach as I write to you. WOW! I want to always have this feeling when I think of you babe. Its my honor to always make you feel the same. I think its important to always date each other no matter how long we've been together or married. We have to always put the work in to keep each other interested babe.

That's what I'm afraid of when you come home. I know you said a thousand times over and over again that you wouldn't, but its super easy to get drawn into the outside world beyond your family. I never want you to lose sight of what's really important, ok? I love you so much and I've become really over protective of our relationship. I'm not crazy, however, I am crazy over you Adore. I'm super nuts about you babe, you are truly something special. Everything about you turns me on babe. Damn! I just wanted you to know how much I look forward to spending every waking moment with you my love. Goodnight babe." (5/24/22, 7:15PM)

Terria: "My Love, lock down!? Damn! Babe, I don't want to exhaust our 5 calls at once like that ever again if we can help it. I'm missing you babe like crazy. I'm a mad woman right now. I don't like this one bit. Honestly, its torture! Babe, I was just thinking about everything we talked about and the merging of our family, and I got super emotional. Like, I got overwhelmed with love and happiness. I never want you to know the feeling of not being unconditionally loved, ever again babe. I got yo ass for life. Just know I'm thinking about you and I love you sooooo much King." (5/26/22, 4:13PM)

Terria: "Peace King, I was young once. Too afraid to give into my desires. Looking back now, I wonder how I resisted, but more interestingly, how I am so free to being face down, ass bare in the air, and ready to take submissive orders from you when you come home.

So often I think about how our first love making session will play out. You mentioned in your previous letter that we might have to 'pull over and FUCK in the car, as soon as we get in and the doors shut'. Lol! That probably would be the first time I'd cum super fast. I had an orgasm just thinking about that moment driving home one evening. Anyways... this is how I picture us making love for the very first time.

Today is the day my husband gets out of prison. We're both so very anxious, happy, emotional, and just so overwhelmed with the thoughts of actually getting to see, hold, and touch each other for the very first time. I fly out, check in at the hotel and shower. I get dolled up just for you babe, I'm looking hella good bae. Lol!

I lay your clothes out on the bed. I bring your Gucci 77's, Gucci belt, cargo's, Ralph Lauren boxers and undershirt, your

Rolex Oyster Perpetual, (Day-Date 40.) Gucci socks, diamond earrings, and your dark gold chain.

I'm in a rented Benz, headed to pick my husband up. I pull up and get out the car. OMG!!! I see you walking out the gate... you see me, I run towards you like I've never ran before, straight into your arms. You immediately dropped your belongings on the ground, grabbed me with both arms, and we hugged each other soooo tight. We held on to each other for dear life. We could've made a river with the tears that rolled from our faces. 'Let's get to the hotel babe, you need a shower'. Lol, I sarcastically implied. To be continued...." (5/29/22, 10:50PM)

Terria: (Continued) "I can hear you turning off the shower... you wrapped the long bath towel around you before coming out to seduce your Queen. Without any panties on, I assume the position, ass in the air and face down. You kissed my ass, 'stay right there, still and quiet, and don't cum until I give you my permission,' you stated to me firmly.

You knelt down behind me, and started to admire how my outer pussy lips were phat and juicy enough to suck on. You lightly rub your finger over my clit, as it slightly poked through. You calmly tell me to 'lean back some more'. You stick your tongue out, and as I leaned back, my pussy landed right on the tip of your tongue. You start to lick my tight pink pussy. Still faced down, ass up, and now my ass is moving up and down with every flick of your tongue. Honestly, I was already wet just from the anticipation of you finding me in that position.

My deliberate deep breaths helped slow down my explosion, forming from your determined tongue. You started kissing the back of my neck and rubbing my clit at the same time. I didn't know how to hold back my orgasm, or my involuntary moans that escaped my throat. So good... so unexpected... I took your towel off and you laid on the bed. I held your hard long dick in my hand and stroked it up and down, inviting your balls into my mouth instantly made you super hard. I kissed you deeply at the base of your balls, and smiled as you tensed up in pleasure. I could feel myself dripping wet from my unresolved orgasm.

I continued to kiss your balls... then I took your full length dick in my mouth. I felt you deep in my throat... OHHH! Massaging your balls with my mouth, sucking on the tip of your head, and teasing you with little bites drove your ass insane. Then, in a rhythmic up-and-down-in-and-out motion, your moans made me wetter, and wanting to take it a step further. I lick pass your balls, and laid my tongue right over your asshole. 'Let me lick it babe,' I demanded softly. I turn on my back and tell you to, 'sit on my face'. I suck and spit on your long hard dick. I stick my tongue out and slide back and forth, from your balls to the crack of your ass.

I could feel your thighs tense, indicating you were close. In and out, as deep as my throat would allow, finally... you exploded in my mouth. I sucked in as I pulled up and pressed my tongue hard against you. You held on to the side of my face with one hand. You tried to tap out but I went on a little longer, just for a little bit of naughty torture. Then... I swallowed your cum... yummy.

'Oohh shit, BAE! You know I wasn't ready to cum yet'. You laughed out. You got up to get my phone off the tripod (where we recorded ourselves) and we watched in awe. As I laid next to you with my leg over yours, you took my hand and placed it on top of your dick and said, 'I owe you'. You put the camera back on the tripod and laid me on my back. I passionately whisper in your ear, 'I love you Adore'. I softly bite the side of your neck as I rub both of my hands through your scalp. Your dick got hard all over again, you motioned it up and down on my phat pussy lips... teasing me, then you quickly removed it.

You got a hold of my ankles and tucked them under your knees, setting them firmly in place. You slowly slipped your big dick head in my tight wet pussy, I let out the loudest moan. You turned up inside of my dripping gushy wet-wet. I had to catch my breath. You brought your full weight down on me, kissing my neck and nibbling on my hard brown nipples drove me crazy.

The look on your face assured me that you really enjoyed how my wet tight pussy, gripped around your throbbing big dick. You slowed down just a little and pulled my legs apart spread eagle, you hammered into me hard and fast. I lifted my hips onto you so that I could feel that thrust against my clit, as my orgasm arose. I let go of your body, reached for a pillow, and screamed into it, 'SHIIIIT!'

Simultaneously, your thrusts became more intensified... my tight wet pussy greeted your young soldiers immediately. Your home cum'n felt tremendous." (5/30/22, 12:08AM)

Nika: "Hello. Got your message. I'm here if you ever need to talk as well. If we can find mutual grounds, then I'm open to being friends. Just not interested in being anything more simply because we're not compatible, as you stated. At first, I was in denial about it, but you were telling the truth. We're literally two different people, with very different views when it comes to certain things. Our strong personalities, strong willed demeanors, & the alpha within us, clash to an extent that things get out of control.

Its like a battle that I find no purpose of fighting. I want to thank you for opening my eyes & mind to a lot. Thank you for the value you added to my life. You're a good person, I won't take that from you. I really do hope your days have been in your favor and are going by quickly. I will continue to keep you in my prayers. God bless."

Terria: "Peace King, I just got back in the office from picking up my divorce papers. WOW! I can't believe its done. Its finally done. Well, I hope your day is going well. I just wanted to let you know that I've picked up my divorce papers. Forgive me if I don't seem too excited, but deep down I am. I just have a shift in energy since this morning. I'm just feeling sad right now, because it seems like our future together is so uncertain. I'on know? But anyways I guess I'll talk to you latter or whenever you can call." (6/6/22, 3:19PM)

Terria: "My Love, let me start off by saying I truly apologize for making you feel not included. I've read your letter and I receive it. I never want to make you feel alone and not included in any way, even if I am upset. In order to build our empire it takes team effort, and you're definitely a team player. Babe, I don't know anyone that has your energy or can even match your energy. You are out of this world. I'm proud to say you're my husband, partner, best friend, and my everything else.

You possess so many characteristics, which made it easier for me to fall deeply in love with you. You're intelligent, handsome, ambitious, motivated, optimistic, determined, loving, honest, caring, and giving. It doesn't stop there, that's just a few.

You have that swag, that SAUCE, that shit that make people want more, and if they blink, they might miss out. Lol! You leave people wanting more. Any woman would want to be with you, and any man would want to be you. So yea, Imma be all over your ass when you get home. Lol! Them hos can look but don't touch. Don't even think you're going to be giving out friendly hugs and shit. If you do, yo ass better think again. Lol! Shiiiiiid, that ass is mine. Lol!!! Allllllll mine!!! You hear me bae???

Anyways, back to what I was saying, lol! Listen babe, I'm going to trust you to do exactly what you said you were going to do. I'm not into micromanagement, so you don't have to worry about me calling you every 10 minutes checking on you. But yo ass do have to check in at least every few hours when you're out of town, you know? I know we're going to get on each others nerves sometimes, but I don't think I can be away from you for days at a time.

Especially if you're talking about being away from me more than a week at a time. Bae, I've never been a clingy person. In fact, I've never been the affectionate type, but you bring it out of me. I've never in my lifetime been more excited to love another man. I just want to love you and only you nonstop, do you hear me? You damn right you're a KING! Trust I know that babe.

I know what I have with you. That's why I'm so crazy about you babe. Your light is a force that only you can carry. I want to spend the rest of my life with you and ONLY YOU

ADORE. There's no other man that I'm sleeping with, talking to, or entertaining.

That's why I get furious when you bring up these accusations, that's insane to me. Can't no man compare to you, in or out of prison. I love the fact that I really have a reason to continue to stay celibate and pure for you babe. You deserve to have a woman that's true with a clean mean pussy ready to fuck your brains out. Yaaaaaaaas!!! I can't wait til my husband come his slim fine ass home so I can smother him with all this love'n. I got you babe." (6/7/22, 12:15PM)

Terria: "My Love, I'm sitting in the living room reading over some of your old letters. My pussy is drenched for you. I can't help but to imagine sitting on your face with your tongue out, rocking my pussy back and forth on it. You start to flick the tip of your tongue on my hard sweet clit. Damn that feels so good... let me ride your tongue... yea, just like that babe.

Don't you dare move, let my juices drip all over your face and right into your mouth. Now come here and give me kisses, let me suck on your tongue and lips. Damn babe, your dick is standing at attention, slap it on my tongue... yea, just like that. Your dick is dripping, here... let me catch it in your mouth. The head of your dick is waiting for my mouth to open wide and let it enter, as far as it can go. Let me deep throat that big dick until I start to gag.

Spit is dripping from my mouth, down my lips, and onto your lap. I'm sucking on that big ass dick, good too bae. Let me slurp them juicy ass balls in my mouth. I'm sucking on your balls and stroking your dick at the same time. Don't cum yet babe, I want to ride your big hard dick. I get on top of you, it slides right in my hot dripping pussy. Uuuhhh!!! Shit, that dick feels soooo good babe.

That's my spot right there bae, my phat ass is bouncing on that dick. There's a huge wall mirror in our room, allowing you to see for yourself how good I'm riding your big dick. You take both of your hands and grab my ass cheeks, spreading them apart enough to view the goodness of my love pouring and dripping all over your dick. I bounce up and down rapidly, 'turn your ass over so I can fuck you from the back,' you demanded firmly.

I obeyed you without hesitation, you started pounding my pussy dumb hard, hitting my g-spot wildly. My own loud moans made chills run up and down my spine. 'FUCK ME-- FUCK ME-- FUCK ME!' I screamed uncontrollably out of pure pussy fuckstration. I couldn't hold it any longer, I drenched your dick with my gushy-wet cum... I showered your dick with love. I quickly got on my knees and sucked on your dick with posthaste. Shortly after, you showered me back with all of your yummy love, redecorating my face." (6/9/22, 5:45 AM)

Nika: "Hey! I'll be home at that time, just give me a call. But yeah I figured you sent the 2nd message before you received my response. Its all good, I've forgiven you for everything, but I'd still like to keep everything on a friendship level.

I'm just really focused on me forreal this time. I got goals to hit & most importantly I gotta get my financial priorities bk in order, which has nothing to do with you. Its like I have a plan, I begin to execute the plan, then something ends up happening. It never fails. This time I prayed hard on everything. I'm trusting God. So now I feel better about the near future. I'm not complaining but stating the facts.

You being incarcerated didn't stop how I felt about you. All I cared about was you and the deep connection we had. The happiness I felt when I saw your name on my caller ID. The unconditional love that I had growing for you that I was ready to fully express to you. I needed you and wanted you. Then you start saying we're not compatible and all that other bullshit, making me feel worthless and hurt. I was sincerely hurt, that's why its hard for me to let it go. Like I forgive you, I really do but that was too much for me to handle.

I would never do that to you, make you feel less than, or mentally beat you down. You were a priority in my life. I looked forward to hearing from you every morning. It was hard adjusting to not hearing from you. With prayer and shifting my focus, I got over it & quickly. I couldn't lose myself once again into someone. Maybe in the future if we're both available we can try being more than friends again. I know you probably wonder if I miss you. Yes I do. I miss everything about you. Especially missed you when we stopped talking.

I was hurting from our situation, grieving to my cousin, and facing other issues all at once. If I just had you to talk to, I know for a fact I'd have been able to deal with ANYTHING, because that's what you do. I had to turn to my strength, God, and make some decisions and get myself together.

I'll always be here as your friend. We always said if we didn't work out, we will be friends. I'm not going back on my word. You're a good person, I'll never take that from you. Don't let anyone else tell you differently. I know you've been around violence your entire life & witnessed some unfortunate situations. Don't let that stop you from being loved the right way by someone who genuinely cares for you." (6/16/22)

Terria: "Hello, if I decide to answer the phone in the morning, please-please-please do not bring up marriage. Please don't! That should be the furthest from your mind Sir. If you start anything with me tomorrow, I'm going to hang up the phone and put my phone on DO NOT DISTURB, for sure. You sound like my brother, and he's a grown man still blaming everyone for his short comings." (6/16/22)

Terria: "Dear Adore, I could use this time to be very negative and wish nothing but the worst for you, BUT I WON'T. I could call you nasty names and really hit you below the belt, BUT I choose not to. You actually said something that kind of clicked, which was, something like, why I'm 'fuck'n with someone in prison?'

You mentioned something like that and then it clicked. You're absolutely right! Finding you was not intentional but you're right, I can do so much better than you. You're selfish, shallow and completely out of touch with the outside world. Please don't ever call me again! The only person you love and care about is yourself. You are very mentally abusive and you need a really crazy dysfunctional, argumentative woman to be with you, and that's not me.

I really want to go off in this email and really say some shit. Buuuuuut, I'm better than that. I'm the better person because I don't have to cut you with words. Usually I'll start to cry as I write, but this time its totally different. I'm over it and I'm over this toxic relationship. We're like oil and water, we just don't mix.

Some people are just meant to be in your life for a season and that's what I believe this is. Now that we've established we're not going to be together, we can both move on. Trust, you will be the first and the last person I will ever talk to in prison. I never in my life want to ever go through this again. I get hit on and asked out a lot and maybe I should entertain the idea of going out on dates. So thanks for telling me I could do much better than dating someone from prison.

I'll put everything in a box, tape it up and sit it in the garage, and maybe 10 years from now I'll open it and go down memory lane. Lol! I'm feeling good right now because deep down I know we are not meant and I'm ok with that. My mister right could be the next guy that asks me out, I mean... who knows. I'm going to transfer you the rest of my stamps because I don't plan to write you after this.

I will delete Jpay all together after this message. I just want to make sure you receive this letter first. I usually never have regrets, but I regret ever believing you ever loved me. I do believe it was all an act to get what you want. I'm sure I'm not the only woman you've done this to. I know this was a lie, and a way for you to live through me, once you are released from prison. You used me the entire time.

What's so crazy is that I don't even know why or how we started to argue? That just means it was about something so small and stupid. I don't want to think like you, I have my own mind. That's why you're in there and I'm out here. Lol! DUH!!! And that's the truth.

If you like it or not, that's the truth and honestly you can take my comment how you want to take it, because you're not my problem anymore, so your feelings are irrelevant. I'll be glad to give your ass back to the streets. You have been institutionalized and there's no way of changing that. You're going to always have that jail mentality. You will NEVER be able to be in a normal healthy relationship because you don't allow yourself to love and trust your partner. You are a true loner and that's how you will always be because you will push everyone away. Peace!" (6/20/22)

Terria: "Hi Adore, I hope all is well. I thought I'd check in on you to see how you were doing. I don't harbor any ill will towards you at all. I'm not that kind of person. I'd never want to hurt you in any way (mentally or physically or even emotionally). Anyways, I've been feeling bad lately knowing you took down your dating profile for me and we're not even together anymore.

If you would like, maybe I can pay the cost to get it put back up. Lol! I never want to stop you from being happy, (yeah right) even if its with someone else. It'll hurt but I know what it is and I'm a big girl, I can take it. Its a part of life, and heartache will always be a part of the equation, you know? But if I can help in any way to get your profile put back up, just let me know. Best, Terria." (6/23/22)

Terria: "You said something a couple days ago and it stuck with me. You told me, I 'need to have a closer relationship with God'. I agree wholeheartedly. I mean, he is the one who created a path for us to meet in the first place. No matter how intense our arguments get, I can't take away the fact that God has put us together for a reason.

How can I ignore that? To really be transparent with you, I don't even own a bible. I'm ashamed to even say it. I was raised in the church. My parents made sure we all had our own bibles. We used to be at church all summer long too. I need to reconnect with God, and I will. I will make sure to buy a bible sometime this week, pray more and read my bible more. Not just read it, but also practice the word.

You gon see bae. I'm going to make some changes in my life that's going to benefit our relationship/marriage in the most positive ways. Its going on 10PM and I haven't received your evening call, so I guess I won't be hearing from you until hopefully tomorrow morning. Be safe and just know your Queen admires you, loves you, cherishes you, and thinks the world of you. I love you babe." (6/27/22)

Terria: "Hey babe, sending you more pics. I was so turned on sucking on that cucumber, I had to have a session babe. All I could picture in my head was how good your dick taste. Just to see the look of satisfaction on your face made me super wet and horny. I was ready to spread my pussy open like a flower and let you taste how good my honey is. I want you so bad bae.

I want you to pin my legs back and deep fuck me good. Passionately kiss me while your hand is around my neck, don't stop babe. Turn me over, now put your phat dick back in my dripping wet pussy that's yearning for you. Smack my ass hard and hear me shout my King's name. 'ADORE, fuck me babe, that's right, my tight juicy pussy, you know you like that shit! Stop! Let me spit on your dick and suck it some more. That's my dick, and I can do what I want with it, as long as I'm satisfying it. Let me taste your love babe'.

You start to fuck me some more and all I can say is how fuck'n good it feels. I'm bout to cum all over your dick babe. 'Yes, yes, yes, babe! Now get the lube and let it drip down the crack of my ass'. I demanded you. You gently put the head in and I gasp in all pleasure. You stroke the head of your dick in my ass, as you inched in deeper I began to scream and moan. 'Relax', you calmly replied, and I do just that. I can't help but to pull the sheets and bury my face in the pillow while moaning louder than before. 'Babe, you're doing so good,' you whispered softly. The more strokes I encountered, it became less painful.

Now I can feel how roc hard your dick is inside my ass, its making me moan more louder with pleasure. My asshole feels so good to you, and your cum all up inside my ass felt soooo good to me. Damn babe, I really can't wait to have our first love making session in the physical. That's gon be some high level intensity fuck'n right there. Lol! Fareal! I'm gon be all over your ass like white on rice. Lol! Its 11:22 PM, and I'm off to bed my love. I'll talk to you tomorrow. Kisses!" (6/28/22)

READ THIS ENTIRE BOOK
READ THIS ENTIRE BOOK
READ THIS ENTIRE BOOK
READ THIS ENTIRE
READ THIS ENTIRE
THIS ENTIRE
READ THIS ENTIRE BOOK
READ
READ THIS
READ THIS
READ THIS
GOD
LOVE
BOOK
FREE
BOOK
READ THIS ENTIRE BOOK READ
READ THIS ENTIRE BOOK
READ THIS ENTIRE BOOK READ

Here are a few questions I respectfully asked Terria, her answers seemed sincere... what do you (Readers) think?

Terria: "Peace King, I've answered all of your questions as you've requested. Please know that each of my answers were genuinely thought about and answered with honesty. Peeling back layers of who I am is not the prettiest because being vulnerable hasn't been normalized where I'm from. So I hope you can appreciate this. Lol!

#1. Have you ever had sex with ANYONE (male or female) during your 'marriage,' or in between your 'separation,' HONESTLY? No I have not.

#2. I am an 'heterosexual' male, what do you consider yourself? I guess I would say bisexual, woman.

#3. How long have you been into 'lesbian' porn? Wow! I would say since 2010. I can remember the day I started watching it and where I was when I was watching it.

#4. Do you consider yourself a 'lesbian'? No.

#5. Have you ever been a part of anything sexual related that was 'recorded' for 'private' purposes, or placed on the internet for 'free,' or for 'currencies'? No.

#6. Within your life, have you EVER accepted any gifts or money from ANYONE, (male or female) in return for sexual favors, HONESTLY? No.

#7. Have you ever 'danced' privately for ANYONE, (male or female) for 'gifts' or 'money,' HONESTLY? No.

#8. Have you EVER given ANYONE oral sex, other than your x husband, (male or female) HONESTLY? No. Honestly, I didn't start giving my ex husband head until 2 years into our relationship. I wasn't a fan of oral sex at first.

#9. Are you concerned about what people think about you, HONESTLY? It depends on who the people are. When I go back home to (the state I was born and raised in) my friends there know me inside out, but my friends in (another state) don't know me like that, they think they do but they don't.

If they ever come to (the state I was born and raised in) with me to visit, they will see another side of me. These are friends that have known me for over 25 years, so I do care what they think. So, the opinions of the people I know here in (this current state) don't hold more weight than my family and love ones back home. The bottom line is this, I'm going to always do what makes me happy regardless of how someone may view or disagree with the decisions I make.

I used to want to please everyone at one point of my life, but the older I got, the more I realized... the more I try to make everyone else happy, I'm the one suffering. For the past 2 years, I've been told by a few of my friends and some family members, that I'm going through a 'midlife crisis,' because I've changed a whole lot. Its not a 'midlife crisis'. They're just not used to me saying 'NO', all the time, and not giving a shit about their feelings all the time. I hope this gives you clarity.

#10. Do you find it easier to lie, or harder to tell the truth, HONESTLY? This is a really good question and I'll try to answer with much transparency as possible. For me, its hard for me to do both. I have told lies in the past, to either protect myself, someone else, and benefit from. I know you're wondering what the hell I'm talking about right? Well, I've told a lie or two to my parents to cover up stupid shit for my sisters or brothers, but my parents knew better. When my dad would give me that look, I would spill the fuck'n beans on everyone. I've lied, and when my conscious starts to get to me, I've always came back and told the truth. I like to hold myself accountable because its a part of my growth process.

Now, have I done that in every situation? No, I haven't. Reason being, the person I must've told the lie to, I probably wouldn't never see or talk to again. To really be honest with you, trying to be the picture perfect child was one of the hardest, fakest, unrealistic things I ever had to do.

It really took away my true identity as a person. I always had to pretend to be someone else. I was so confused as a young adult because I felt like my identity was lost. Who am I? I didn't know because I pretended for so long, it took years to find, recognize, and love the real true Terria. I'm so very proud of the person I am today. I know who I am and where I'm going. I love how strong driven and fierce I am.

#11. Do you currently have ANY conversations with ANYONE (other than myself) by phone, via computer, etc., (male or female) that are attracted to you sexually,

HONESTLY? I would say that I have flirted back with men on Instagram in my DMs. I've never given out my number. I communicated with a few guys through Instagram. I've never considered it to be serious but it felt good to be noticed.

#12. Have you EVER had sex with anyone outside of your own race, (male or female) oral included, HONESTLY? No I have not.

#13. How long have you been attracted to women? I think I was 19 when my cousin and I was club hopping and we went to this one club (we didn't know it was a gay club at the time). I couldn't understand why I was getting hit on by women? I looked up and saw 2 guys in the corner kissing, I was like ooooooh! Lol! I was asked to dance and I enjoyed it. I was super scared to give out my number, because, again, my dad would have gone crazy if he knew I had those kind of feelings for the same sex. So I kinda just pushed those feelings down, and never really thought of it again until now.

Adore, I hope this gives you some kind of clarity. I've never been this open to anyone before. This is me and who I am as a person and not the person that wears many hats." (6/29/22)

Nika: "Hey! My bad for missing your call this morning. My alarm was set for 10AM. So I missed you by a few minutes. Hopefully we speak again, & hopefully the chaos in there has calmed to a minimum so you can get back to normal. I know it gets hard for you sometimes in there.

I pray for you. Crazy thing is, no matter what the obstacle is in life, it always gets harder before the blessing. I look at it as God's way of truly testing our faith, and to see if we will keep moving forward or give up. I know God already knows the answers, so maybe He's just showing us the outcome of our faith in Him. All I know is that I pray your time flies by and you're home with your family very soon. You're a good dude. I can tell you've progressed a lot in life despite spending time in prison. Your body may be locked up but I know for a fact your mind isn't.

So many people roam this earth daily who are prisoners of their mind. They have no peace, can't sleep, can't eat, and barely can make it to the next day. So I'll take a cell any day over being a prisoner of my mind. So remember to always keep your head up and stay moving forward. I know you're probably saying that's easier said than done. I get that, trust me I do, but you have to remember that you have God. So you will be okay, as long as you truly trust in Him and put your faith in Him.

I hope that I was able to lift your spirits and give you a different outlook on the things currently taking place in your life. You know I've been going through a lot. More than what I tell you. But I keep trusting God and doing my part. I pray and put in the work. Prayer or even faith without work is dead. When you feel like the world is on your shoulders, just start to think of everything that you have to be thankful for. Concentrate on the good." (6/2922)

Nika is fading away....

Terria: "Baaaabe!!! I'm missing yo ass immensely. I worked out, came home and took a shower, and now I'm sitting in our living room with my neon pick leopard print panties on, a white crop shirt, with my nipples on the hard. Lol!

That's nothing new. Lol! Anyways, I like how you describe what you were doing and wearing in your cell. Thank you for that. I would appreciate if you would share things like that often. Its not every day that I get to receive current pics of your handsomeness. When you share little visuals like that, it makes a big difference babe.

I've listened to 'H.E.R.' loving that song 'Lights On,' and I visualize us in our bedroom with the lights on of course. I'm mesmerized by each other's beauty and imperfect bodies. I love you bae. I'm in love with you bae. I love how passionate, creative, loyal, honest, ambitious, loving, intelligent, smart-as-hell, confident, etc. I can go on and on my love. There's so much to you. What I love the most about you King is how you refuse to be defined, by the prison system.

Babe, I don't want to think you have to immediately start making money as soon as you get out. I don't want you to get frustrated or feel defeated if profit don't come in as fast as you anticipate it. I'm still going to ride hard with you, and for you, always babe. I got forever. I'm not saying this will happen, but I just want you to know where I stand if it does.

I love you to pieces babe, your wife forever." (6/30/22)

Terria's super hyper sexual ways, soon became the exact reason my 'video visits' were canceled for one year straight.

Of course, Terria's wrongs are NEVER A BIG DEAL whenever she's the reason behind the consequences. To be completely honest... I wasn't even the aggressor when Terria decided to incorporate sexual gestures (via) through a video visit, at me. Trust, the moment my video visits were canceled for a year, Terria could care less. Terria's lies became the normal... and she sucked at it.

Terria: "I just got off the phone with you not too long ago. Not sure what happened but the phone hung up and it was not my doing. Anyways, I understand that you are upset with me and I get it. Do you resent me for this? You expressed the way you felt and I set and listened. I took heed to every word, but for you to go on about me being the cause of you not being able to have video visits was unnecessary. I apologize for being the reason why you're unable to have video visits. I regret trying to please you in every way possible, and now we're paying the ultimate price of doing something against prison policy. Lol! Does this make you feel better, I'm sure it doesn't but what else do you want me to do?

I'm not a self centered person at all. I have made sacrifices and lots of them. Its been times when I don't even feel like talking but I do, because I love you and I want to always be the one to put a smile on my your face. I have my good days and my bad days, just like you, I deal with it in my own way.

I don't know how to date someone from prison, and make them feel as though they're actually here with me. I don't know how to have a long distance relationship. I don't know Adore, but I've been taking it day by day, and I've learned a lot from you. I am who I am and you are who you are. Its up to you, if you want to be in this thing with me, knowing that it will take time to get where you need me to be, and vice versa. I'm all in but are you?" (7/9/22)

Nika: "So I got on Jpay to fill you in about what's been going on lately. However, you deleted me. So its useless to even get into it. I can't keep dealing with someone who continues to delete & block me every time things don't go their way. I'm out here fucking grinding 24/7, I was raised not to depend on no man. Idc how much my daddy and family spoiled me, grinding and hustling is instilled within me. I don't sit around & make excuses, I get off my ass and make shit happen.

Its the only way to make it. I know you going thru shit in there, but I'm going thru shit out here too. When I'm focused, I fall back from everyone and everything. Its not just you that I don't talk to every day or consistently, its everybody. This is just me when I'm on grind mode. I had to stop playing with myself and get fucking serious.

Its known that when a person is like this, they lose a few friends along the way. I just didn't think it would be you again! But it is what it is Adore. You will never understand me. You just don't get it, when we are on the phone we never talk about anything. It's not like it used to be. We just sit there, and it's the same questions being asked and the same answers given, the remaining 15mins its nothing said. I can't continue to allow you in and out of my life, I just can't. If you want me out, say it. Don't pull these crazy ass deleting stunts. You really can't understand where I'm coming from, and that deleting me shit is old and I'm done with it.

I don't tolerate that kind of disrespect. Like I was a fool once, trying to get thru your head. I thought we were good for each other, I was ready to try and work out what we had started, and you showed your black ass on me. I won't be a fool again. So let me know ASAP. Anyways, I hope you're good and God bless you." (7/10/22)

Terria: "My Love, I can't see myself getting another divorce babe. I just can't! I want to be your wife forever. I take marriage very seriously, that's why I was with my ex for so long. I wanted to make sure I did everything possible to save our marriage, but it just didn't work out like that, and I'm ok with that, obviously. Lol! Hello! Lol!

I want to be your slut bitch in the bedroom and sophisticated lady when we're out in public. BUT, I'll be your little slut too if we want to have a quickie session when we're out and about. Lol! I will be all you need and want babe. Honestly babe, I thought I'd be able to shake you off after our very first big argument. I thought I'd be able to block yo ass and not think twice about it but I was totally wrong. Clearly! Lol!" (7/10/22)

Nika: "I thank God that I put my guard back up. Idc that you're in prison. When I wake up, I have so many missed calls & text messages. I don't even call back or respond. In my past, I did talk to some clown ass dudes because I was young, dumb, and just living life. But I don't entertain clown dudes anymore. Oh yeah, I'm very far from ungrateful but I'm definitely stubborn. Lol.

You got it, you win. I'm not going to degrade you or put you down. I uplift black men and black people in general. I know I'm a blunt person and very straightforward. I never find ways to water down what I have to say, especially when speaking facts and while having a real heart to heart. I haven't met a man yet that can handle that shit. Y'all pride always get hurt. Never my intent. Maybe your pride got in the way or you're just an asshole. Idk, not going to take the time to even find out.

Honestly, I didn't expect to be deleted from the email list. I was excited that I was finally about to send you an email simply because of what I had done & accomplished. I was excited to share that with you, but once I opened the app and saw I was deleted... all that excitement went out the door. You know, I had went the extra mile to try to make up for the delays, missed calls, or whatever. I wanted to share that with you in the last email, but didn't because you blocked me.

I had ordered some designer lingerie that wasn't too revealing. I took pictures in the outfits just to send to you. Next week I start training for my contractor job, which I do from a computer. I was going to let you know that I'll definitely be available more since I'll be working from home.

I know you don't need it, but in August, I would've been in a financial position to help you out whether you need the help or not. Last thing I wanted to share with you is that I signed the lease to a bigger house, so I'm moving by the end of the week. Those funds I got approved for will go towards the new house since my lease here is up this month. Anyways Adore, I wish you the best in life. I'll still send prayers up for you. I hold no grudges or have any hate for you. God Bless."

Nika fades to blackness....

{"The real art of conversation is not only to say the right thing in the right place, but to leave unsaid the wrong thing at the tempting moment."}

(Dorothy Nevill)

READ THIS ENTIRE BOOK
READ THIS ENTIRE BOOK
READ THIS ENTIRE BOOK
READ THIS ENTIRE
READ THIS ENTIRE
READ THIS ENTIRE BOOK
READ THIS ENTIRE BOOK
GOD
LOVE
BOOK
FREE
READ THIS ENTIRE BOOK
READ THIS ENTIRE BOOK

Terria: "If I scream at you then I'm being disrespectful. If I'm trying to stay level headed then I'm disrespecting you. I'm convinced there's nothing I can do to make you happy. You're super angry and there's nothing left for me to do.

I'm completely done! You can now pursue your options." (7/11/22, 7:25PM)

Terria: "I'm not upset at you for wanting to be done with our relationship. However, I am hurt but it is what it is. I'm sure its hard being in there and I'm out here and having to trust my every word. To think about it, its a lot of trust that's not easy to put into someone.

So I get it, and the way things have been playing out lately... I definitely can see your point of view. How things may look, to be honest, I would be upset and hurt as well. You want it to be over and I'll respect your wishes. Anyways, I'll stop here and let you go. Stay safe and always keep your head up." (7/24/22)

Words of the Philosopher, David's son, who was King in Jerusalem.

ECCLESIASTES, C7 v 26-28

{"I found something more bitter than death--woman. The love she offers you will hold you like a chain. A man who pleases God can get away, but she will catch the sinner. Yes, said the Philosopher, I found this out little by little while I was looking for answers. I have looked for other answers but have found none. I found one man in a thousand that I could respect, but not one woman."}

Terria: "So can you picture us sucking your big ass dick? You fuck'n her from the back while she's eating my pussy. Can you see it babe? I'm attaching pics, how does she look to your eyes?" (7/25/22, 4:03PM)

Terria: "Hey babe! Have I told you how incredibly proud I am of you? Well, if I haven't, let me just say, King, I'm so very proud of you. Your work ethics are impeccable and I love how you're so reserved in your own kinda way. You have many things that differentiates you from the rest my love. I want you to know that you contribute a lot to our relationship, and I couldn't ask for more. I see you trying babe, and all I can say is please continue to try and so will I.

We all have room for improvement, and I strive to be a better me each and every day. I want to, and I also want to show and prove to you that I can and will be your everything." (7/31/22, 8:30PM)

Terria: "Adore, what a waste of calls earlier. I could tell you all the things that you do that bothers me but I won't. All I'm going to say is, please give me my space when I ask for it. I really don't like how you take me out of character. It takes a lot to get me that upset and this is your second time doing it. Usually I would cry or get a lot of butterflies in my stomach. I had a few, but not like I normally would. This is a clear indication that I'm slowly starting to detach from you. I know if this continues, eventually I'll be checked out of this relationship.

I told you I'll never leave you and I meant it, but I wouldn't have no choice but to leave if you continue to push me away. I'm not gonna be somewhere I'm not wanted. Right now I believe we need to give each other some much needed space. This is my way of trying to save our relationship. I'll elaborate later. I'm wishing very bad Ju Ju on yo ass. Like I was hoping you would hit your pinky toe on the corners of a table or bed. Then I was hoping you had bad diarrhea and couldn't make it to the toilet in time. LMFAO!! Goodnight." (7/31/22, 9:15AM)

Terria: "My Love, you really know how to piss me off, buuuut you do a damn good job making sure I'm happy and feeling loved. Listen babe, I know you have to be super innovative in your ways of showing your love for me. I get it, and I know how much you wish you were home to contribute more to our future and happiness.

I know you want to be the provider, and I know you can be. I believe in you and I want you to know that I'm going to always rock ten toes down for you my love. As you always say, 'we have to stay prayed up,' and I honestly believe that. I want to connect on a deeper spiritual level with you.

Our relationship isn't easy and I think we'll have a better understanding and respect for each other's individuality once we build on our spiritual connection. What do you think babe? I'm ready, so I kinda need you to guide me through the Bible babe. Will you?" (8/1/22, 8:34PM)

Terria: "Peace King, it feels so good to have and receive good energy babe. To have that from you in the top of the morning is a blessing, and it assures me that my day will be a positive and productive day. Thank you my love. We're approaching our 6-month anniversary and I want to continue to build and elevate with you my love.

I want us to be able to celebrate our 6-year anniversary. We have a lifetime to go my love. Babe, most of the time I'm really fiend'n for you. Anyways, I have several emails I need to attend to my love. Ttyl. Gimme kisses daddy. Love always, Your wife & best friend." (8/4/22)

Terria: "My Love, I love spending my mornings with you my love. You know it really took some getting use to first, but I've grown to actually waking up to you... even if its via phone. We are growing as 1 each and every day, and it feels so amazing. I want to spend the rest of my life with you Adore. So we made a promise to each other not to ever leave and to stick it out, through thick and thin. WELCOME TO THE WORLD OF MARRIAGE my love. Lol!!!

I'm going to make this really quick because I have to get back to work, I'll talk to you this evening.

Sincerely, your wife and number 1 supporter, always." (8/5/22, 2:30PM)

Shalonya: "Good morning Adore. I know you don't know me and I know this is very-very weird and awkward, but I was watching this show called 'Love After Lock Up,' and I just decided to see what the hype was about. When I went on those sites, so many inmates popped up it was crazy. Your pic stood out and I wanted to just try this out to see? I've never done nothing like this before. I don't mind being a friend for conversation or for those hard times in there. So my name is Shalonya, and I'm from Detroit Mi, I have 2 kids and I'm currently in school for RN. If you can get phone calls you can call me at (number) hope to hear from you soon." (8/6/22, 9:06AM)

Adore: "Good morning... hopefully this ecard will put a lil smile on your face=0). I'm typing from the main computer, therefore, this message won't be too long... I'll call you soon... enjoy your day." (8/7/22)

Terria: "My Love, I really want to thank you for being the man of my dreams. When I tell you, your words speak life, please believe me. Your words speak volumes babe. You always encourage me to be a better person and to be pushed to my full potential. I'm just in awe of you. Sincerely, your Queen." (8/6/22)

Shalonya: "Hey Adore, hope all is well in there, thanks for the e-card. They letting y'all get more tech savvy in there huh, Lol? Well here are a couple pics, talk to you later." (8/7/22)

Adore: "Hey Shalonya, hopefully you enjoyed your weekend, and hopefully the kids did as well. Errbody seemed to be enjoying themselves when we talked=0). Hopefully this week will bring forth some good energy and many Blessings for you. Take your time out there... and remain focussed on your goals... continue to strive for, ELEVATION!

As for myself... Elevation has become a Lifestyle for me, real. I must admit... its good to hear your voice... I have yet to receive your message/pics, therefore, I'm just sending you this message beforehand. I'll most definitely hit you back once da pics hit. Stay up... I'll call you first chance I get. I'm sending this message to you with Love and Respect, sincerely, Adore." (8/7/22, 10:52PM)

Shalonya: "Hey babe, I'm glad we had our morning talk this morning. I'm liking that we got a little connection already. Lol, and I'm glad you been so strong holding on because you don't deserve all that time babe." (8/8/22)

Shalonya: "Hey babe, my phone has been acting up all day, call me on my other phone (number)." (8/9/22)

Terria: "You asked me several times if I made any sex videos and I continued to say NO! And every time I said NO, you would bring up old conversations we had months ago. And then you start to accuse me of making sexual content for the world to see when I don't answer my phone.

Every time I don't answer my phone that's what I'm doing. I'm out here bad. I'm fucking everybody. I have several sex tapes out and I'm sure you'll see them once you get out. Daaaaaamn!!! ARE YOU HAPPY NOW??? This is what you want to hear so bad so there you go ASSHOLE!!!" You're FUCKED UP IN THE HEAD!!! DISRESPECTFUL ASS FOOL!!!

Just because you was in the streets slangin yo nasty ass dick in mothers, daughters, and friends, doesn't mean I was on my back letting trifling ass niggas like you inside of me. If I would've seen yo ass on the street, I wouldn't have even given your ass a glance.

There's plenty I want to say but I'll let this sit right here for now, ASSHOLE!!! (8/10/22, 9:18AM)

PROVERBS C20 v 22

"Don't take it on yourself to repay a wrong. Trust the LORD and HE will make it right."

Adore: "Terria, you no longer have my Blessings, for anyone who is not for me IS TRULY AGAINST ME! That now includes you, therefore, may your karma be not only your own destruction, but also your conquering defeat. Terria, you have disrespected me for the last time... so now you can go around and pick out fake pieces about me to TRY and make yourself look good in front of others, something you have clearly became accustomed with. Trust, and please believe GOD knows you, and I now know YOU HAVE SOME REAL DEMONS INSIDE OF YOUR DEMENTED HEAD! You display the worst 'love' of all, FAKE LOVE!!!!

YOU ARE A FAKE!!!! All you try to do is puppet master people, buy 'love'. You try to purchase people's affection with money or gifts and then think you can control them and boss them around, NOT!!!! THAT'S NOT HOW REAL LOVE WORKS!!!!

Real love comes from your heart... you don't take advantage of people considering their current situations, so that you can have 'the upper hand'. You were already damaged by your 'x husband'. So now your intent is to get 'payback' from every man you meet, until your own karma catches up with you... and trust me... it will.

Yes, I am somewhat kicking myself in the ass (but not for long) for allowing you to waist 6 months of my time... considering I could have been with a REAL GOD FEARING WOMAN, MOVING FORWARD IN THE RIGHT DIRECTION, without fake intentions, and may GOD still Bless me with a TRUE GOD FEARING QUEEN, ON HIS OWN TIME, AMEN!!!!

A True Queen, that hasn't already been completely destroyed and damaged. A True Queen, that doesn't have to tell petty lies to TRY and make herself look 'flawless'. A True Queen, that doesn't go around TRYING to make herself 'superior' over others. A True Queen, that will Love honestly from her heart, for 'better' or for 'worst,' with HER SAME PURE HEART, AMEN!!!!" (8/11/22)

Shalonya: "Hey babe, I be thinking about you eating my pussy, and me deep throating your dick. I love sucking dick, only if we got that connection. Feel my throat sucking all that dick, and I'm going to breath through my nose and let all the spit and slob just trickle down my face. Then I want you to explode all down my throat, I also love getting my ass smacked. I can picture you smacking my ass and fucking me hard and deep from the back while I squirt and cream all on your dick babe." (8/11/22)

Adore: "Hopefully your day is going productively... it was good to hear your voice again this morning, and your laugh is priceless=0). I'm currently on lockdown in the cell, we should be able to come out at 6:30PM, after headcount. Meanwhile... I'm sitting in here thinking about you and listening to some throwback SWV, picturing my lips kissing yours... enjoying how your beautiful eyes look as I began to kiss your beautiful face, neck, and soft breast.

My tender kisses make it hard for you to hold back your juices... and MY BIG THICK LENGTHY DICK instantly gets hard from every soft inch of your phat super soft chocolate ass. I slowly lay you down on the bed and make my way down to your feet. Your eyes are now glued to my every move. I quickly throw both of your legs back and began to kiss your feet and inner thighs. Your nails feel soooooo good massaging through my thick natural locks.

Your moans began to intensify as my lips slowly find their way straight to your sweet honey hole. The smell of your soft sweetness made it easier for my lips and tongue to embrace your phat tender pussy lips. The introduction instantly drove you insane. Your moans were uncontrollable. It didn't take long for you to notice the difference from 'the rest' and now the best.

I waisted no time speeding up the tempo as I continued to eat, kiss, spit on, and suck up all of your juices mixed with mines. I destroyed your pussy... I ate you completely out... disrespectfully, in the very best way. You couldn't help yourself from throwing your drip'n wet pussy all over my lips, tongue, and mouth with posthaste speed.

I sucked and swallowed on you deeply. Your moans and direct eye contact assured me that your love was about to come raining down on me... and it did. 'Shiiiiiiiit Adore... um bout to cum Babe!!!' You shouted uncontrollably. 'Cum in my mouth... that's right, cum in my mouth Babe, gimme that pussy'. I taunted at you, while simultaneously continuing to splash my soaking wet tongue all over your drip'n gushy-wet-wet.

'Fuuuuuuuck, Adore... that shit feels soooooo good Babe!' You moaned loudly, as you made direct eye contact with me. Your juices splashed down wildly and redecorated my face and beard. I made sure I sucked and slurped up all of your drip'n love... then I slowly made my way back to your soft sexy lips and passionately kissed you Queen. We both enjoyed the taste of Pure-Real-Deep-Black-Love, at its apex.

'I want you King... I want you right now King'. You softly whispered in my ear along with your sweet tender kisses. My manhood instantly got SUPER ROC HARD as you slowly made your way down to your King's manhood... kissing my neck first, and then slowly kissing my chest. Tell me about the rest when time permits you Queen." (8/11/22, 4:31PM)

Shalonya: "Yes babe, I got your message and sorry for missing your call this morning. I was dreaming about waking up in the mornings with your dick growing inside my mouth. I'm sucking on your dick sooooo good that you wake up moaning and grabbing the back of my head while my spit is running down the shaft of your dick.

Please don't hold back that big morning build up nutt, I want you to release that nutt all down my throat. Its warm too! And I'm not spitting it out, I'm swallowing every drip drop of your nutt... yummy daddy... you taste so good. Your dick remains rock hard, and you tell me to 'get on top'.

So I get on top, but backwards though, so you can see my heart shaped black phat ass riding the shit out of your dick. I'm riding your dick standing on two feet, ass cheeks clapping very loud as you smack my ass and choke me from the back. Then you flip me over and just finish me by drilling the shit out my tight, juicy, creamy wet pussy. The slurping smacking noises from my drenched pussy drives you to fuck me even harder... 'ahhhhh' I moaned from your pleasures.

'I love you... ahhhhh,' I moaned overwhelmingly. It was that very moment you busted a huge load of your seeds all in my pussy. You kiss my soft sexy chocolate back, on down to my ass cheeks, then you came back up and we tongue kissed romantically. You ended the kiss with your lips on my forehead, we cuddled up in each other's arms dreaming and talking about how good both of our loving is to one another. We smoke a phat wood and fall back to sleep." (8/13/22)

Terria: "Happy Anniversary KING of my life! I'm so grateful to be on this journey with my forever husband. To be able to build with you is always a blessing. Thank you for choosing me to be your forever Queen. I'm so very proud of you and I'm super proud to call you my husband/King. Babe, do you know how our day would've went had you been home? Well let me tell you my love. You would've been awakened by my soft juicy lips, suctioned around your dick head. My tongue gliding up and down the shaft of your dick. Damn babe! Is that a vein I see popping out on the side of your big thick dick? You're super hard and excited to be getting some of the best sloppy toppy from your wife.

I'm spitting and gagging on your beautiful ass dick, and you're just laying back enjoying it as I'm starring into your eyes. I'm tasting all of your love in my mouth. Now let me get on top and ride that dick babe.

My pussy so wet and my clit is big and hard. You're nibbling on my nipples, squeezing and smacking my ass as I ride your big dick with rhythm. I love it when you cum in my pussy, I lift up off your dick so you can see your cum sliding down my leg. Now, let's get cleaned up bae and go have brunch. Wear something casual but fitting for the occasion. 'Damn you smell good babe,' I whispered softly in you ear.

I just want to undress you and go at it again, but damn, we have to make our reservation as planned. We decided to take your CLS S550, because it suits the occasion, besides... its sexy just like us. Lol! We make it to our destination safely, which happens to be this beautiful grown and sexy lounge. They're playing all our favorite old school (late 90s, early 2000s) R&B hits. There's several couples on the dance floor. 'Come on babe, dance with your wife.'

We dance to Tevin Campbell's (Can We Talk) while laughing and whispering sweet nothings in each other's ears. I'm so turned on by you, I tell you to 'meet me in the restroom'. Five seconds after I walk in... you walk in and lock the door behind yourself, lift me up, and sit me on the countertop.

I have on some crotchless panties, so you spread my legs, stick your tongue out, bend down, and please my sweet tight pussy. You then yank me off the counter, bend me over, and start fucking me hard and deep. Placing your hand over my mouth helped conceal my loud moans. 'Don't cum yet babe... decorate my mouth,' I demanded you suddenly.

I suck on your dick till you fill my mouth with your love. I open my mouth widely, so you can see with your own two eyes as all of your love disappeared down my throat. 'Ok babe, let's straighten ourselves up before we go back out,' I quickly stated. We calmly walk out together, back to our table and order our food... colossal shrimps and grits. The conversation was great, we enjoyed each other's company, and the food and music was superb." (8/14/22, 12:13PM)

Shalonya: "Good morning babe. I'm hoping you're having a good day. I can't wait until you call me so I can hear your voice, LOL. You know what's crazy? I was cleaning up yesterday and that song 'fuck faces' came on by 'Scarface and Too $hort.' I instantly thought about yo freak ass, well here's a picture collage of me, hope you like it." (8/17/22)

Terria: "My Love, Oh! How you have me on cloud 9, smile=0). I really enjoyed spending time with you my love. To be your Queen, wife, and best friend is an honor babe, so THANK YOU. You are an amazing King, husband, and best friend. We are truly blessed Adore. I haven't been able to focus at work today because all I could think about is YOU, US. Lol! I'm dead serious bae. Lol! I'm so ready for you to be home and take off with you. I'm ready to wake up to you each and every morning, and greet you with sweet stinky breath kisses.

Lol! My heart is forever yours pumpkin. My boss just came in looking hella crazy. Lol! She looks like she's been attacked by pitbulls. Lol! Wish I could take a pic. Hehehehehe! I'm about to see what's going on and try to get some work done babe. I'm really hoping you'll change your mind and call home this evening bae, but if not, I guess I'll talk to my handsome, sexy, intelligent, intuitive, charismatic, God fearing husband tomorrow morning. I love you babe." (8/18/22, 2:15PM)

Adore: "Damn... so now I see why you went straight into defence mode when I told you I was going to call you after '10PM,' my time. You obviously already had your plans made. I guess it was meant for me to inquire about calling you after all, time does 'tell.'

Then I called you back to back, and you still hadn't made it to dance class yet? 'Traffic,' okay, whatever, but wait... there's more, then I call during your 'dance class'. Remember, you told me it started at '6:45PM,' your time, the normal, and ends at '7:45PM,' which is 8:45PM my time. So why no answer at approximately 8:50, 9----through 9:15PM, my time? Then... approximately 10:50 through 11PM, my time?

But I guess in your mind it doesn't matter, because as long as you answer the phone at 6:30AM, your time, I'm cool with whatever you tell me, NOT! Whatever it is or whoever it is you are doing, is it really worth losing me? LORD knows I'm trying everything within my willpower to hold on.

I wish you could've heard yourself earlier on the phone, you were trying to make up every excuse in your book for me not to call you tonight. You lied right in my face Terria, and its crazy because I told you that I needed to talk. You inconsiderably disregarded me. I could see right through your fakeness, and then you actually tried to use 'reverse phycology' on me, talk'n bout I be 'putting monkey wrenches in things'. You are waaaaaaaay too smart for me Terria, I tell ya, LOL!

However, there is no excuse for tonight that will ever make me believe you again. You played yourself out. The only thing that can even began to help this situation at this point is if you step up and be woman enough to TELL ME THE TRUTH, PERIOD. The crazy shit is all you had to say is 'I'm going out,' etc., but you fumbled AGAIN. Instead, you actually had me calling you back to back several times, clownish shit.

The trust that I put into you is not reciprocal from your behalf, with me. YOU FAIL HORRIBLY AT BEING HONEST!!! You try to make things seem good, but behind closed doors you struggle with real demons. The sad thing is I feel like I know exactly what you struggle with. What's sadder is the fact that you won't even be woman enough to talk to me straight up, which makes me feel like I can't TRUST YOU!

Terria, I've continued to TRY to give you multiple lanes to be authentic with me, but yet you continue to disrespect and violate my trust. There is no way within this world any REAL WOMAN that TRULY LOVES her man/husband, etc., would EVER let her phone ring as many time as you did tonight, PERIOD.

Now I'm at a point where I have to start checking myself, its not even you at this point. I most definitely don't want to hold you up, from continuing to do whatever it is or whoever it is out there that's making you 'happy'. 'Happy,' to the point that you miss an inexcusable amount of my phone calls, and continue to tell lies to me.

Whoever it is... maybe that's the person or people you need to spend the rest of your life with. If you are reckless enough to risk us for that... then it wasn't meant to be in the first place. So you see Terria, its not me. ITS YOU!!! This is a reflection of your own sloppiness, your own inconsistent 'love'. I keep telling you Terria, I DON'T KNOW HOW TO LOVE PART-TIME!

Not sure what lie(s) you will make up next, but I don't even need to hear them, save it... anything other than THE TRUTH, miss me wit it, real. If you just slow down for one second and really think about what you are doing... just really think about the damages that you are creating.

Really look at the love and support I shower you with EVERY DAY. You are really willing to ghost me completely for some fuckoff time, are you serious? So that's all I'm worth to you is some fuckoff time? Well guess what Terria... you now have all the fuckoff time in the world you need, so please CONTINUE TO DO YOU!

I'm not about to keep cutting myself short from REAL LOVE, by TRYING to love someone (you) with my all, only to be toyed with and lied to, THAT'S NOT REAL LOVE!!! At this point, you have clearly showed me that your other options are way more important than I am".

(8/24/22)

Terria: "Peace King, I apologize for not answering my phone. I heard everything you said this morning and I can see why you were hurt, upset, and angry. Anyways, I don't expect for you to understand or agree with some of my actions. Of course you don't believe me, it hurts me to hear how upset and hurt you are. Adore, I truly don't have a problem letting you know if I'm going out or not. I had absolutely no intentions of staying after dance class but it happened. The only time I've ever slept out, was at my sisters house. I have my own way of doing things, but it will never be where I'm disrespecting you or our marriage." (8/25/22, 1:19PM)

READ THIS ENTIRE BOOK
READ THIS ENTIRE BOOK
READ THIS ENTIRE BOOK
READ THIS ENTIRE
READ THIS ENTIRE
READ THIS ENTIRE BOOK
READ THIS ENTIRE BOOK
READ
READ THIS
READ THIS ENTIRE
READ THIS
GOD
LOVE
BOOK
FREE
BOOK
READ THIS ENTIRE BOOK
READ THIS ENTIRE BOOK
READ THIS ENTIRE BOOK

Terria's rope of lies began to thin out... fast. I will admit, Terria had semi-mastered the art of manipulation. How much more do I allow myself to take, at what point do I let go of Terria's rope of lies and allow her to continue to hang herself, by herself? After Terria's 'vacation' back from Porto Rico, the energy between us became more toxic. Regardless, I continued to play 'possum'.

Terria: "My Love, I enjoyed every minute we were on the phone while I was on vacation, so please don't think for one second that I didn't. At least now my best friend (her name) can see how much of a role you play in my life. Not just any role, but the most important role as being the man that I love in my life. It was important to me that she really understood the love we have for each other. Our love is real and safe, and she gets it. Lol! I didn't care how much they clowned me for being on the phone with you. I'd get clowned everyday if it means I get to be with you forever. Lol! That's you calling me as I'm riding in the Uber. I'll end it here. I love you soooooo much babe. Your wife forever, MRS. TERRIA HSAAF." (9/4/22)

Terria: "Adore, I'm assuming me not picking up the phone for you got you in your feelings. I didn't answer because I clearly told you I was sick and suffering with a horrible headache. I made the executive decision to put my phone on silent so I can take a shower, tried eating some soup, and I took some thera-flu.

I went to bed early and woke back up after 2AM, made another cup of thera-flu, and I didn't wake up until a little after 12PM, the next day. I still was feeling horrible, so later on that evening I went to urgent care. I had a sinus infection, that's why my throat, ears, and head was hurting so bad.

I would've answered had you called after lunch, just to give you an update on how I was feeling, but I wouldn't have been up to having long conversations because of my condition. I don't want nothing to do with you, I've blocked your number.

Please don't ever send any letters to my house nor my mom's house, because I submitted a form to the postal service to block and return any of your mail, if you do decide to send any mail. So please don't because it will get returned back to sender. Please reach out to my mom via phone once you are released, so you may retrieve all your letters, paintings, cards, pics, etc., because I don't want any reminders of you. I've tried and I gave you my all, well at least what I can give, given your situation. Be Blessed." (9/15/22, 1:26PM)

Terria: "Dear Adore, I was immediately taken away with how intellectual, charismatic, and sophisticated [hood] (I mean that in the greatest way ever) you were. I remember saying to myself, 'damn, I've never met anyone like him before'. Then it became more real, the more we spoke to each other, I was on cloud 9. It took me some time to fully open up to you, but I did. Trying to commit suicide was one of the worst things I've ever done to myself, and especially my family. To have my son find me like that tore him up inside, to see his mother non-responsive, I'm paying for that every single day and so is he.

After today, the back and forth, and you outing me like you did, there's no way we could ever be together. We could never be friends. Lose my number and pictures. Start fresh with someone else. I don't want any parts of you. You are officially DEAD TO ME! You don't exist to me. You are nothing to me anymore. I wouldn't even spit on you if you were on fire.

GO FUCK YO SELF BITCH!!!!!" (9/18/22, 7:07)

Adore: "Peace Queen, I will admit... all of this negative energy is really bringing out some disturbing sides with BOTH OF US! I hope and pray we both make it through this. You made yourself clear though, you don't want anything to do with me, say less." (9/19/22)

Terria: "So I just finished writing you a long ass letter just now and it got deleted from Jpay. I hate this stupid app. I don't have time to write another letter like that so I'll just summarize what my deleted letter said:

Basically I was apologizing for some of the things I said in my most recent email to you. I'm sure you received it this morning as I had received yours as well. To be more specific, I want to apologize for saying I wouldn't be friends with you or spit on you if you were on fire. I would definitely put the fire out. Lol!!!" (9/19/22, 10:37AM)

Terria: "Peace King, Adore, you almost loss me forever. I've been through a long 20 year relationship with someone that drained the energy out of me, to a point where I thought I'd be better off in the ground. So when you say, 'now you want to run,' that's not me running. That's me saving myself from falling back into that rabbit hole that I refuse to go back into.

When I left my EX, I didn't know nothing about living on my own. I was scared of the unknown. As time went on, I started to really get to know ME, love myself more, and create boundaries for the people in my life, which includes my family, friends, and kids. I really didn't know who I was as a single parent until I put in the work to build myself back up. Now I am a way better version of who I was before." (9/21/22, 9:32AM)

Terria: "Thanks for giving up on me, on us." (9/25/22)

Terria: "But after all this, I still love you. After all this, I'm still going to be loyal. After all this, you still will be the only man that has my heart. After all this, I'll still wait for you. I guess we can't be together while you're in prison, and I have to except that. You still and forever will be my everything. I don't know if this is goodbye, but whatever it is I hope its not forever. Be Blessed." (9/25/22, 2:58PM)

Terria: "My Love, I'm just getting out the shower. I have my fan on and I'm oiling my skin from head to toe with lemon grass oil. It smells so good. I know we're not on the best of terms right now, but I'm super horny and all I can think about is riding my future husband's big dick. I'm going to rub my pussy and think about you kissing me there, there, there, and of course there too! My clit is super hard and my pussy is dripping wet. I want to slap you and tell you how much I want you to fuck me and punish me. I know you're super upset with me right now but just know I love you more than you'll ever know. Good night." (9/26/22, 7:14PM)

Terria: "Babe just know I'm going to always be yours and you'll always be mine. There is no in between. This is what its going to be forever. This huge hump is temporary. One day soon, we will be laughing at all the times we cussed each other out and broke up. We will be able to enjoy the rest of our lives together in the near future.

THERE IS A LIGHT AT THE END OF THE TUNNEL. We have to be strong enough to overcome this obstacle. Together we can do and overcome anything babe. Please understand, I'm not your enemy my love. I'm going to ALWAYS take your side. I'm going to ALWAYS defend you." (9/26/22, 9:00PM)

Terria: "I was really hoping you were going to call me back so I could tell you how much I love, want, and need you. Please stop acting like you don't love and want me. You know we wouldn't have NO problems if you were home. You don't never have to worry about if I'm going to let everyone know what's up with us. Trust me, I know what I'm doing, so let me do it on my time. I'm sorry for making you feel like I'm ashamed of you because that's NEVER been the case.

I wouldn't have told the one person that I love the most, which is my mom. I always look for her validation and she's given it to me. Everyone else will be made aware in due time. I'm not hiding you my love. I love you and I love what we have and I want to always protect it. I can't bring everyone in on what we have, until I know for sure our relationship is planted on solid ground. As far as the foundation goes, everyone's opinions, questions, and negative juju can do damage to our relationship before you are even released from prison.

These are the same people who will judge and think they know you, based on your current situation, and right now I don't want to deal with that shit babe. Please Adore, you don't want Pandora's Box open. This is something I hate to bring up because its stupid, and my people are good at degrading anyone that they feel are not up to par. So there you go." (9/26/22, 9:27PM)

Adore: "Not really sure when you may receive this message, hopefully sooner than later. Terria, thank you for absolutely wasting my time. You are another reflection of why I shouldn't get 'married,' nevertheless while I'm incarcerated. I hope you find that super tough soul (man or woman) that can put up with your lies, lies, and more lies. You are as fake as they come.

Not really sure why you even decided to have my custom logo tattooed on you??? Now would be a good time to have it removed, ASAP, like YESTERDAY!!! You are a disgrace to REAL BLACK WOMEN... or any woman for that matter.

Having 'sex' is your answer to everything, especially when things don't go your way. Terria, you need some real professional help, seriously. Also, no matter how much you may think that you are 'superior' to some people, (incarcerated included) YOU ARE NOT!!!

I have more respect for a homeless person living on the streets. I will love that same homeless person with every inch of my heart and soul, sincerely, why, because having 'money' or being more financially stable over others does not make you 'superior' over anyone, and it NEVER WILL!!!

So now is the time for you to stop putting fake names on my email account, now is the time for you to find someone else to entertain your circus act with, because as far as I am concerned... your show is OVER! Life goes on, I hope and pray that you find your real self, and just know that its okay to be alone in your process of trying to find your real self. You shouldn't want to bring others on your unbalanced journey with you, especially by trickery.

Take care of yourself out there, seriously." (10/30/22, @ 3:02PM)

Terria: "Just received your emails and even your most recent email from 10/30/22. That was pretty hard to read but I can't change the way you feel, so it is what it is. To say I'm, 'a disgrace to Real Black Women' is pretty harsh and it stings only because its coming from someone I loved and cared for immensely. I apologize for my part in the demise of our relationship.

Just for the record, I haven't created any fake accounts since the Jessica account. I swear, you don't have that to worry about with me. I'd rather not know if or when you're communicating with someone else.

We're not together so its none of my business. I'll keep this Jpay up til tomorrow afternoon, and then I'm deleting your name and this app. Its time for both of us to have a fresh start. You won't be able to email me after tomorrow afternoon, and you won't be able to call me after Thursday. I'm getting my number changed. As far as the tattoo, I'll be getting it covered soon. I'm going to New York next month, so it'll probably get done after I come back.

I'll send your nephew a pic of the tattoo once its been covered. This is my final email to you. I wish you the best!" (10/31/22, 3:31PM)

Terria: "I love you and that will never change, together or apart. It is what it is and I'm going to take it for what it is. Stay up." (11/01/22, 9:00AM)

Adore: "If we are going to do this the right way, let's not half step at all. Yes, I agree... get that tattoo removed ASAP, before you go to 'New York'. Thank you. WE ARE NOT GETTING MARRIED!!!" (11/3/22, 10:50AM)

Terria: "YOU WILL NEVER FIND NO ONE TO TREAT YOU AS GOOD AS I DID! However, you will find someone, but guess what? You'll be settling because won't no good woman in her right mind ever want to deal with a narcissistic man like you. Your mouth and your fucked up ways will never allow you to reach your full potential, because you are stuck in your ways.

You haven't done shit for me. You were the only one that benefited from this so called relationship. All you ever gave me were orders and fuckn headaches. I can't believe I waisted my time, money, and tears on your sorry ass. You're not worth it! FUCK YOU BOY!!!!

WITH YO BITCH ASS!!!! You act like a fuck'n peasant nigga!!!!" (11/3/22, 5:04PM)

Adore: "Terria, you are a compulsive liar... then you try to make up fake bullshit to make people feel sorry for you. You even lied about having 'kids'... and you lie soooooo much that you actually forget what you say, and what you type. You need some real professional help.

If you think for one second that I am going to feed any further into your poppycock, YOU ARE CRAZY!!! I can't trust you with a glass of water, so what makes you think I can trust you enough to actually live with you in the same household??? NOT!!! You have absolutely no regards for my life in prison, or anybody's for that matter. So why should I expect anything to be different with you when I'm released from prison???" (11/4/22, 1:43)

Terria: "Once I feel like you received this email, I will delete you FOREVER! Now you've gotten me to a place where all I'll have for you is a strong dislike. I wouldn't say hate, only because I really don't hold hate in my heart.

The love for you will disappear sooner rather than later. Lesson learned. Never get with a inmate, run for the fuckn hills. That's what everyone was telling me, and I wish I would've listened. I could've saved myself the trouble of getting fucked over by you.

-Your Enemy." (11/5/22, 9:38PM)

READ THIS ENTIRE BOOK
READ THIS ENTIRE BOOK
READ THIS ENTIRE BOOK
READ THIS ENTIRE
READ THIS ENTIRE
THIS ENTIRE BOOK
READ THIS ENTIRE BOOK
READ
READ THIS
READ THIS ENTIRE
READ THIS
GOD
LOVE
FREE
READ THIS ENTIRE BOOK
READ THIS ENTIRE BOOK
READ THIS ENTIRE BOOK

After going through sooooo much drama and negative energy with Terria, I had reached the apex of tapping out. Considering the fact that my profile on Meet-an-Inmate was about to expire, I had decided not to renew it.

Not only were my emotions damaged... so was my heart, soul, and spirit. There was only one thing left to do, which was the exact thing I started with, praying to GOD.

I took more time to pray up to GOD. I kept my faith super high, I never gave up on finding "true love", I just decided to " let go and let GOD." I asked GOD to help "guide me in the right direction," on THE ALMIGHTY'S TIME. Therefore, I completely relinquished trying to find "true love" on my time.

ECCLESIASTES C3 V1

{"Everything that happens in this world happens at the time God chooses."}

ECCLESIASTES C3 V 11-12

{"He (God) has set the right time for everything. He has given us a desire to know the future, but never gives us the satisfaction of fully understanding what he does. So I realized that all we can do is be happy and do the best we can while we are still alive."}

I can't even front... I had completely relinquished on trying to meet any women on "Meet-an-Inmate.com," and the last thing I was concerned about was renewing my profile. Therefore, I just took that new extra time to catch up on my music writing, painting, drawing, etc.

{"Fishing is a lot like love. It takes patience and faith to land a great catch."} (Marilyn Turk, Niceville, Florida/ Guideposts, April 2011)

Nola: "Hello, I saw your profile on Meet-an-Inmate.com, and to me, your profile reads simplicity and peace, but I want to know the story your eyes tell. I sent pics so that you can put a face with the stranger messaging you, (me).

I'm interested Mr. Robinson. My name is Nola by the way. I'm 36, born 4/20, I have 5 wonderful kids, four girls and one boy. I'm a native of South Carolina. I know we don't know each other but I would like to be your friend." (12/4/22, @ 12:06AM)

"Here we go again, Terria play'n more games." I thought dreadfully to myself, as I noticed the name (Nola) that mysteriously popped up on my email account. By now I was all burnt out on playing kiddy games with Terria, therefore, my initial approach to "Nola," was of uncertainty???

Adore: "Hello 'Nola' Lol, not really sure what all or who???"

Surprisingly, Nola was easy to talk to, and considering the turmoil I had just escaped from with Terria, learning that Nola was actually a real person was 'a breath of fresh air'. A few days after Nola had reached out to me... my Meet-an-Inmate account expired.

However, there was no way possible I could see myself ever being serious with Nola. After all... she had already married three times, divorced all, five kids, three different 'baby daddies,' and a plethora of other problems that consisted of too many of her own challenged demons. Nola's weaknesses quickly became concerning factors for me.

We both had been through our fair share of rough struggles. We both experienced real life trenches. I could easily recognize some of the familiar demons Nola struggled with, reason being, because I once struggled with some of those same demons. It was a very painful experience... I turned to GOD... AKA,

THE ALMIGHTY, whom answers my prayers. I changed my old ways.

PROVERBS C20 V30 {"Sometimes it takes a painful experience to make us change our ways."}

It was something super special about Nola that I just couldn't figure all the way out? On the other hand, Nola struggled with being honest about important issues. Like most people that lack self discipline with controlling their physicals, understandable, after all, being in a huge world filled with beautiful people, how could I really blame her? My true concerns, were in regards to getting Nola to be comfortable telling her truths to me, beforehand. Whichever decisions she decided to make, "bad" or "good," BE HONEST AND JUST OWN UP TO YOUR OWN SHIT!

The first couple of months were VERY DIFFICULT, and the only conclusion I kept constantly coming up with:

SHE LIES BECAUSE I'M INCARCERATED, PERIOD.

Argument after argument after argument... no matter how much I disapproved of Nola's lies, cheating , etc., my vision of the True Queen I saw Nola as... NEVER CHANGED.

PROVERBS C22 V12

{"The LORD sees to it that truth is kept safe by disproving the words of liars."}

The holidays went fairly smooth... as well as the new year, which I enjoyed celebrating with Nola and her kids. Nola's kids opened up a piece of my heart that overwhelmed my spirit and soul. I instantly fell in love with the joys that Nola's kids possessed. Regardless of some of the negative energies Nola struggled with, she truly loves her kids. That fact alone made it super easy for me to fall in love with Nola, and love her kids as if they were my own biologicals.

Nola: "Seems like a shift is happening, I'm here and prepared for it. Meeting you has been a blessing to me. I'm not the most talkative person, I'm pretty closed off and I have my reasons. Meeting you in this manner forces me to take it back to the basics, slow down, and thoroughly enjoy us.

I was mentally preparing myself to be alone, rock out with my kids, and build for us. Then BOOM... 'ADORE!' I look forward to your calls, hearing your voice, and our awesome conversations. My days are easier with you. I think of you often, and I find myself smiling, laughing, and just reflecting on what we talked about.

I have been through a lot, I have done a lot of things, the lessons I've learned forced me to get to know myself. I know who I am and I want out of this life. I have faith that we can continue to build on a strong foundation. Thank you for pouring into my cup. Thank you for being the King that you are, I love that and I love you!

We talked about openly communicating the pretty and ugly things, and I have been needing to say this, I have seen guys string women along, talk to different women in their harem, and even show pics and details comparing them. I don't want to entertain those spirits. I know you probably looking crazy, but I have to be straight up because I believe in you, I believe in us.

I want more only if we can both keep it transparently real with one another, if not, you still have a platonic friend in me. I got a surprise call from you, and what you said about my patience made me say, 'this man is bold'. I like that realness, you turned big purr on, she got moist. Just put me in my place and you might be right. I mean patience is a virtue. I needed to hear that." (2/14/23, 9:51PM)

Nola: "Babe, thank you sooooooo much. I appreciate you more than you know. You are always speaking positivity into me, motivating me, and on my ass holding me accountable... that means the world to me. You give me what I need King and I love you for that.

You came through and picked me up when I needed you the most. You are giving me exactly what I need, your positive energy, and mental strength, which helps me avoid the bullshit. Again babe, I appreciate you for coming through for me today. I LOVE YOU!!! LETSSSSS GOOOOO!!!" (2/22/23, 4:14PM)

Nola: "Darling, I want to make love... but this time, I thought we could try something a little bit different. I want to do all the 'work'. I want to please you... try not to move voluntarily except for accessibility movement, unless you are shifting us into a final position, so that you are able to penetrate me just before you climax.

I am sitting up in our bed, with my back against the headboard... naked. You are naked and laying on a long body pillow across my lap. The pillow is there to help raise your whole body up, now I have full access and neither one of us struggle to maintain our positions. Your head lays comfortably under my breasts. 'Open your mouth babe,' I calmly implied. I placed my left nipple in your mouth, as if I was nursing a baby. My pussy started to twitch... I was on the verge of releasing.

I moan in pleasure, as you continued to blissfully torture me. I deliberately bear down and let my legs squeeze together, hard... hard enough to encourage the orgasm that wants to explode.

I slightly move under your body as I push and relax... push and relax... push and relax... until I can't relax any longer, I burst... all over your long and thick dick. My body shudders beneath you, you suck on my tender nipples just a little harder and bite down slightly. We both moan out, as I give into the first of what will be many orgasms tonight.

Your broad shoulders are accessible for kissing... so I do. I reach across your body and grip your upper arm, pulling you slightly towards me. You follow my lead and turn partially on your side, making it easier to reach your shoulder that is farthest away from my body. I work my way up to your neck, you relax back onto the pillow again, and lay flat on your back.

My soft kisses continue across your chest, and not closed mouth little kisses. I am letting my tongue play all over your chest... as I work my way downward I pause... deliberately... to suck on your chest nipples. I play there until you moan... we are very in tune with each other. Signals are no longer needed as I slowly work my tongue down your body.

I reach your navel and stop to suckle... your erection is growing. With each kiss and each caress, your dick gets longer and thicker. You reach down to grip your dick and start massaging it, but I quickly stop you. 'No babe, just relax and breathe, let me please you, just relax and breathe,' I softly demanded you.

My soft kisses continue, but when I reach your scrotum, I stop. 'Slide all the way up babe, I want to move to your feet and work my way up,' I calmly implied. Your moans mixed in with a touch of frustration, which highlighted your anticipation. I'm deliberately lengthening blissful sexual torture, and something else lengthened on you as well.

I placed soft kisses on your toes, ankles, shins, knees, calves, and on the inside of your legs, trying my best not to miss an inch of your skin. After I reached your crotch... you moaned in pleasure. 'Turn over on your stomach,' I whispered. You smiled at me and shook your head tacitly implying 'no,' but you reluctantly complied. You flipped over, and the firmness of your erection pressed against my closed legs.

Badly, I am craving the feeling of your long thick dick inside of me. With only the feeling of your erection pressing against me... I cum... harder this time. Once the shuddering spasms of my orgasm ended, both of my legs and your dick were decorated with my cum. Suddenly, you moan and whisper, 'fuck me'.

The moistness from my release aroused you fully, which made for the perfect time to firmly grip your enormous dick. You are thirsty for me to taste you, but I don't. I simply hold your dick out of the way, and calmly make my way to play with your balls with my mouth.

First, I embraced them with my super wet kisses, second, I grip them softly with my mouth and lips, third, I suck on them with all of my suction power. Earnest sucking, as if I were thirsty. Wonder what's making you grip the bedsheets so intensely? Suddenly, I hear you whisper, 'please babe,' so I gently release your balls out of my mouth.

Now, I turn my undivided attention to your dick. Gently squeezing and maintaining constant pressure from your base, all the way to your tip, took you to another level of anticipation.

You partially vent your desperate need to thrust. In a way, I yield to that need. Next, I demand that you drop to your knees... and you quickly obey. Now that your huge dick is at the perfect level for sucking, you place your hands on my shoulders... and I take you into my mouth... with full honors.

Swallow... suck... swallow... suck, I controlled my own tempo, and feeling the tip of your huge dick twitching hard against the back of my throat, instantly made my tender pussy lips throb.

Again, swallow... suck... swallow... suck... you moaned out and squeezed my shoulders tighter. Shortly after... I am finally tasting your delicious pre-cum on my tongue. I put my hands on your hips, to halt your thrusting motion, withdrawing you from my mouth. You moan and nod with understanding. My body is aching to feel you release inside of me.

We shift our positions, now I'm lying flat on my back, you're holding my legs open... smoothly... your body slid between them. Both of our hands ease your dick inside of me... I began to cum at the very beginning of penetration. You continue to slide into me very slowly... I moan, loudly! My hands clench, as I nervously take in your massive shaft. I stop you intentionally, half of your penis rested inside of my wet pussy, firmly.

You smile, and press your full length inside of me again... I moan in more pleasure... it feels sooooo good receiving all of you. I whisper softly to you, 'place your arms behind my shoulders, and lift up slightly,' you quickly obeyed. I take a deep breath... lean back against your arms and deliberately bear down on your dick.

Push, pant, push, pant, push, pant... at last, we slip over the edge together into the ecstasy of mutual orgasms. Our screams and moans became one, as we climaxed together, collapsed together, recovered together, and then... fell into sleep... together. This is the apex of bliss!" (3/7/23, 10:42PM)

Nola: "The kids were gone for the weekend, so we planned a stay-cation, and booked a very nice room at the Ritz Carlton. We checked in, got settled, and ordered room service. After dinner, you sat calmly with your stomach full. I appeared from a near by distance fully undressed.

You watched in awe, then stated, 'crawl over here,' I obeyed. I knew exactly what to do, so I proceeded to unbuckle your pants, take your dick out, and top you off with some sloppy head. Shortly after, you led me to our bed. I laid down first and you placed your nicely fit body on top of mine... gently, you sucked on my breasts.

The more you sucked... the wetter I became, so much so, that I had an amazing orgasm from you gently sucking my titties. You were amazed that I orgasmed from you doing that. Before taking your dick and rubbing it against my pussy, you got in front of me on the bed, looked at my pussy and said, 'damnnnn babe, you're so wet... you're soaked.' You then stood over me and stated, 'lick your juices off the tip of my dick, right now'. I quickly obeyed... and you kissed me afterwards.

Finally, you firmly placed your erected thick dick's head slowly in my pussy... while looking directly into my eyes. Deeper... and deeper... you broke my tender walls completely down... and it felt amazing as well. Tears started to roll down my face uncontrollably, from being so emotional. We both reached our climax and orgasmed simultaneously... speechless." (3/22/23)

READ THIS ENTIRE BOOK
READ THIS ENTIRE BOOK
READ THIS ENTIRE BOOK
READ THIS ENTIRE BOOK
READ THIS ENTIRE BOOK
READ THIS ENTIRE BOOK
READ THIS ENTIRE BOOK
READ THIS ENTIRE BOOK
READ THIS
READ THIS BOOK
READ THIS ENTIRE BOOK
READ THIS ENTIRE
READ THIS ENTIRE BOOK READ
THIS ENTIRE BOOK READ
THIS ENTIRE BOOK READ
GOD
LOVE

The mental and sexual gratification that I shared with Nola over the phone was incredible. I'll give her an A+ on that. Lol. However, I wanted to elevate on a higher level with Nola... starting first with GOD. Trust, that task was not easy, but I had quickly grown to love Nola and her kids enough not to give up on them.

One of the facts about GOD that most people don't know is... you can be yourself with GOD, I mean like... YOU CAN REALLY BE YOURSELF WITH GOD!!! GOD knows everything about us, so we ('humans') can't try to 'trick' GOD. GOD IS OMNISCIENT, which basically means/ GOD has total knowledge; knowing everything.

Also, GOD IS OMNIPRESENT, which basically means/ GOD can be everywhere, simultaneously.

JEREMIAH C23 V23

{"I am GOD who is everywhere and not in one place only. No one can hide where I cannot see him. Do you not know that I am everywhere in heaven and on earth?"}

Adore: "Hey Bae, just got off da phone with you, it was great to finally hear your voice again. I PROMISE I WAS WAITING ALLLLL DAY=0). Bae, I thank you for giving me your words as your bond, in regards to TRUST, paying attention to my ways, what I will stand for, and what I will not stand for. I WILL STAND MY GROUND FOR MY RESPECT, BECAUSE I GIVE RESPECT. Its real easy to let go... but that's not what I want... at all... I really need for you to become ONE WITH ME, the same way I AM ONE WITH YOU.

Basically... in other words, whatever you do negative out there (behind closed doors) does not only come back to haunt you, but that same negative energy reflects back on me. Nola, I'm TRYING my best to keep demons out of your living space, because sometimes you can invite demons in unbeknown. I told yo ass girl... you a lil behind schedule, LOL! I've been waiting on you... still holding my hands out waiting on you to catch up to me, LOL=0). Regardless, as long as one of us has the lead... we will both make it on time, TOGETHER!" (4/17/23)

Nola: "Bae, I was super horny yesterday, it was an out of body experience like something came over me. I had to kill my flesh by praying... and taking my ass to bed, lol.

I ONLY WANT YOU. I'M LOYAL TO YOU. You have become very special and an important person in my life, and our kids. 'Mansion,' or 'hut,' my love for you will remain the same. I'm focused on GOD, family, and school only. If its not about elevating spiritually, pouring into my family (which now consist of you) our kids, and my schooling, I could care less.

I'm coming up on a week of detoxing (weed) and I'm so ready for this lethargic feeling to leave me. How is the book coming along you're writing? I know you're getting it in, I'm very excited about this project. Bae, ain't much going on here, just missing you." (April 25th, 2023 @ 7:57AM)

Adore: "Hey Bae, thanks for setting up that video visit this morning=0). Also, it was great to speak to you again... I really did miss building with you. As you can see, Satan is quick on his feet, however, GOD IS QUICKER, SUPER FACT!!!

So please remain focused out there, WE GOT THIS!!! Trust, I think I am seeing everything I need to see from the people I call my 'friends,' as well... lessons learned. Also, please keep this in mind... I have been locked up for approximately 20 years now. I missed the entire 'search for personal information' about people 'online' wave.

TRUST, EVERYTHING ON THOSE COMPUTERS ARE NOT RIGHT AND EXACT. So please know that if you ever feel the need to 'search' something up about me, you can ask me straight up, PERIOD. I have yet to lie to you, and I'm not going to start. I LOVE YOU, STAY FOCUSED ON US PLEASE!" (4/28/23, 8:21AM)

Adore: "Peace Queen, not sure if I will be able to call back, the phone lines are out of my control tonight. I'm working on the book and TRYING to keep some order in here, NOT EASY with some of these guys. N-E ways, I love you, the first phone that comes open, I WILL TRY TO CALL YOU ASAP. Please TRY to make time for us, first thing in the morning if possible. Sending you all of my love, now and FOREVER. Sincerely, Your KING & Best Friend=0)." (5/04/23)

Nola: "Good morning My King!!!

Today is a new day and I want you to know I appreciate you. I look forward to you being my life partner. I look forward to creating memories together, hearing your voice, seeing your face, laughing with you, and crying together. Just know that you are my King, my best friend, and my soon to be Husband, hopefully. My heart is at peace.

I. LOVE. YOU.

I am committed to you, to us.

You have my loyalty.

You have my love." (5/17/23 @ 6:19AM)

Adore: "Thank you for sharing your energies with me, regardless, 'right or wrong', I AM RIDING WITH YOU, FOREVER, PERIOD. STAND FIRM IN YOUR WORDS AND STOP LOOKING BACK. YOU DAMAGE YOURSELF WHEN YOU DO THAT. SOON... LORD'S WILL, WE WILL BE 'AS ONE'. LEAVE THOSE NEGATIVE PEOPLE ALONE!!! IF THEY ARE NOT TRULY FOR US, THAT MEANS THEY ARE AGAINST US!!!!! IF YOU ARE TRULY STRIVING FOR ELEVATION, WHY WOULD YOU CONTINUE TO RETURN BACK TO KNOWN SINNERS?

2 PETER C2 V21-22

{"It would have been much better for them never to have known the way of righteousness than to know it and then turn away from the sacred command that was given them. What happened to them shows that the proverbs are true: 'A dog goes back to what it has vomited' and 'A pig that has been washed goes back to roll in the mud.' "} (5/22/23, 4:39PM)

Incorporating positive energy into any relationship, friendship, etc., isn't as easy as it may seem, sometimes. However, the fact that Nola and I both worked super hard within our own individual ways to produce healthier communication lanes, made it easier for us to both boon from each other's work ethics towards our future together, hopefully "as one."

Nola: "Yes, we got this! Our past, due to my decisions and actions, were far from perfect. Before December 4, 2022, we never knew each other existed. Neither of our circumstances are ideal, but I loved you from the moment I saw you.

The sincerity in your eyes captured me. I understand. I will communicate with you, I will be honest with you... bottom line is... I'm in love with you and only you. At the end of the day I'm riding with you until the wheels fall off. I will be where ever you need me to be, I love you babe." (6/3/23)

Adore: "Hey Bae, I'm currently in the cell waiting for the doors to pop. I'm reading the XXL mag you got for me. I just made it to Lil Durk's interview. Right off da rip the interviewer asked him: 'How's life right now? What kind of space are you in?'

Lil Durk: 'Great space. Creative space. Thinking space. To myself space.'

Interviewer: 'Why is that, sometimes to yourself?'

Lil Durk: 'I can think better to myself. Not a lot of opinions around. Not a lot of bad opinions around. I had to CHANGE MY CIRCLE. I'M TRYNA WIN'.

Bae, WE ARE NOT ALONE, I TOLD YOU... ERRBODY NOT GOING TO MAKE IT. PLEASE FOLLOW MY LEAD, DO WHAT NEEDS TO BE DONE FROM YOUR END, & I PROMISE I GOT US FROM MY END, FOREVER!!!

Thank you Bae, WE GOT THIS!!!" (6/7/23)

As a child I use to hear adults say "you ain't on your time... you on GOD'S Time." I may not have fully understood the true meaning of that statement back then... but I think I do have some clarity of that truth now. After all... it was GOD that cleared the runway for my super awesome Wife and Kids, to land safely into my arms... on GOD'S TIME, AMEN!!!

ECCLESIASTES C3 V 1-11

(A Time for Everything)

"He sets the time for birth and the time for death,

the time for planting and the time for pulling up,

the time for killing and the time for healing,

the time for tearing down and the time for building.

He sets the time for sorrow and the time for joy,

the time for mourning and the time for dancing,

the time for making love and the time for not making love,

the time for kissing and the time for not kissing.

He sets the time for finding and the time for losing, the time for saving and the time for throwing away,

the time for tearing and the time for mending,

the time for silence and the time for talk.

He sets the time for love and the time for hate,

the time for war and the time for peace.

What do we gain from all our work? I know the heavy burdens that GOD has laid on us.

He has set the right time for everything.

He has given us a desire to know the future, but never gives us satisfaction of fully understanding what He does."

Nola: "Babe I am only 11 miles away from you right now, and tomorrow we will be in each other's presence. I'm currently in the bed watching your show on BET, 'Sistas,' and I am completely lost? I don't know who is who but its interesting and full of drama.

Thank you for riding with me today, you made the trip much easier. I cannot stop thinking of you. I can't sleep but I'm going to force myself as soon as I finish sending this message. I just wanted you to know I'm in the hotel room, and I'm not going anywhere. Also, the phone hung up before I could tell you that I love you, sooooooo... I LOVE YOU KING!!!

See you in the morning at 9am, (video visit)." (6/14/23, @ 10:17PM)

Adore/ June the 15th, 2023, I laid my eyes on Nola for the first time, in person. I was able to see with my own eyes how beautiful GOD made her. She complemented my appearance as well... it was a great moment. Looking directly into my Queen's BIG BROWN BEAUTIFUL EYES, gave me a piece of freedom... a piece of sweet freedom away from this unbalanced prison environment that I had become immune to for the last 20 years of my life, and still counting....

One of the female staff members here at this prison asked us, "how long have y'all been knowing each other?" Nola and I both nervously looked at each other, and replied simultaneously in shy voices, "for a little over 6 months." Another female staff member quickly responded, "that doesn't matter, when its true love there's no time limit on true love." Me and Nola smiled at each other, I cheerfully replied, "AMEN!"

Soon after, the Reverend was phoned in... he gave his Blessings respectfully. Nola and I stood face to face and traveled away into each other's eyes. The Reverend quoted a very familiar passage from THE HOLY BIBLE, regarding to "Love."

1 CORINTHIANS C13 V 4-13

"Love is patient and kind; it is not jealous or conceited or proud;

love is not ill-mannered or selfish or irritable; love does not keep a record of wrongs; love is not happy with evil but is happy with the truth. Love never gives up; and its faith, hope, and patience never fail.

Love is eternal. There are inspired messages, but they are temporary;

there are gifts of speaking in strange tongues, but they will cease;

There is knowledge, but it will pass. For our gifts of knowledge and of inspired messages are only partial;

but when what is perfect comes, then what is partial will disappear.

When I was a child, my speech, feelings, and thinking were all those of a child;

now that I am a man, I have no more use for childish ways. What we see now is like a dim image in a mirror;

then we shall see face-to-face. What I know now is only partial;

then it will be complete ---- as complete as GOD'S knowledge of me.

Meanwhile these three remain:

faith, hope, and love;

and the greatest of these is love."

A few days prior to June 15, 2023, I remembered Nola asking me, "are you going to write your vows down?" I thought about it for a quick second... and replied "nahhh, ain't no way... um come'n straight from da heart. I don't need to write nothing down, that's what you do. Matter of fact, you do yours how you do yours and just let me come from my heart, let me do me." Nola was like, "oooookay." Lol. Maaaaan... I thought I was going to come 'straight from the heart'. NOT! Lol.

The next day Nola presented her vows that she wrote for me... I read it and quickly made it 'universal,' Lol. "Bae, is it okay if we share the same vows?" I asked nonchalantly? "Whaaaaaat... you can't be serious, not you, I thought you was going to come 'straight from da heart,' Lol." Nola replied sarcastically.

"Yeah-yeah-yeah, I hear you Bae, but seriously though... those are the most heart felt words anyone has ever said to me. I love you Queen." I calmly replied, as my tears slowly made their way down my face.

"Are you serious Bae?" Nola asked in awe.

"Absolutely Queen, not joke'n, are we even allowed to share the same vows?" I quickly asked?

"We should be able to, but are you sure you want/"

I cut Nola off before she could finish her sentence.

"Bae, of course, absolutely, what you wrote is perfect. I would be honored to share the same vows that you wrote for me, with you. WE GOT THIS!!!" I responded excitedly.

The time had now come... as the Reverend instructed me to read my vows to Nola first, my heart felt as if it had skipped a few beats. However, I took a deep breath... and calmly proceeded to read my vows to Nola.

June 15, 2023, @ approximately 3:45PM

{"When I first met you I had no idea you would be so important to me. You are my best friend, my human diary, and my other half.

You mean the world to me.

I didn't fall in love with you.

I walked into love with you, with my eyes wide open, choosing to take every step along the way, because I do believe in fate and destiny.

But, I also believe we are only fated to do the things that we'd choose anyway.

And I'd choose you in a hundred lifetimes, in a hundred worlds, in any version of reality.

I'd find you and I'd choose you.

By GOD'S Grace, I will love you and help you, as you lead us towards Christ.

I promise to grow my relationship with GOD.

I will continually seek to love, comfort, honor, respect you, and be subject to you as The Church is subject to Christ.

I commit to encourage and support you.

Continue to be patient with me... as you have, as I continue to set my goals in life, to please both, GOD and you in all things.

I will stand beside you and forsake all others.

I will keep myself only for you, as long as we live.

Sincerely,

Your Husband, Best Friend, and KING, now... and forever....

PROVERBS C3 V3

'Never let go of loyalty and faithfulness. Tie them around your neck; write them on your heart'.

In Jesu's Name, Amen!"}

Now see... whoever said "it ain't no such thing as a happy ending"? Matter of fact, let me call my Wife real quick and see if she wants to add any final words to our 'happy ending'. (Calling... phone rings... continues to ring... and finally, an answer). An unknown male voice answers: " Hello."

Adore: "Uhhhh... my fault, I must've dialed the wrong number."

Unknown Voice: (LOL) "Ohhh shit, I think I know who this is. You that clown ass lame that married Nola, right?" (LOL)

Adore: "Say what, a who da fuck is this answering my wife's phone, and where da fuck is my wife at?"

Deon: "This Deon, you 'ont know me, um just your wife's 'one night stand'. (LOL) She right here though, laid up right beside me. I'ont think she get'n up no time soon either. I just knocked that pussy ooooooout!" LOL!

Adore: "What da... a, what's that location!?"

Deon: "My 'location,' (LOL) you can't be serious, why?

You locked up in da pen, and unless you get out today you gon be a lil behind schedule try'na catch up to me, PARTNER! (LOL) I be lay'n my pipe down from state to state, (LOL) But for right now, my current location the same place you call 'home'. Yeah that's right, um laid up right beside yo bitch, my fault, your 'wife'. LOL! Wait... wait for it... AND YOU CANT DO A DAMN THING ABOUT IT!!!" (LOL)

Adore: "A look bruh, maaaan... you 'ont know me, you talk'n real reckless right now."

Deon: "I know exactly who you are... your name 'Adore' right, your first name 'Adore' right!?"

Adore: "Maaaan."

Deon: "Your first name 'Adore,' and your last name 'Robinson' right? Your last name 'Robinson,' ain't yo last name 'Robinson'? Your last name 'Robinson,' ain't yo last name 'Robinson'? I saaaid, AIN'T YO LAST NAME ROBINSON!? ROBINSON! ROBINSON! ROBINSON!"

"ROBINSON!!! ADORE ROBINSON!!! WAKE UP!!! YOU HAVE A VIDEO VISIT SCHEDULED FOR TONIGHT, AT 8:00PM. DO YOU ACCEPT OR REFUSE, I NEED TO KNOW RIGHT NOW!?"

The loud and disturbing correctional officer's voice awoke me... reassurance that not only was I still incarcerated, but also reassurance that I just had an awful dream, a dream that seemed surreal. Beads of sweat trickled down my face.

Adore: "Sir, may I respectfully ask, who is the visit from?"

CO: "Uhhh... let's see... according to my list here... its frommm... a------ ... oh, here we go, its from a...

'Nola Robinson.' (LOL!) YOUR 'WIFE'!!!!! (LOL!-LOL!)

Made in United States
Orlando, FL
30 June 2025